Geronimo Stilton

THE TEST of TIME

THE SIXTH JOURNEY THROUGH TIME

Scholastic Inc.

Library of Congress Cataloging-in-Publication Data available

ISBN 978-1-338-30619-4

Text by Geronimo Stilton
Original title *Viaggio nel tempo-6*
Cover by Danilo Barozzi
Illustrations by Silvia Bigolin, Danilo Barozzi, and Alessandro Muscillo
Graphics by Chiara Cebraro and Marta Lorini

Special thanks to Shannon Decker
Translated by Julia Heim
Interior design by Kay Petronio

10 9 8 7 6 5 4 3 2 1   19 20 21 22 23

Printed in China   62

First edition, February 2019

Geronimo *Stilton*

THE TEST of TIME

THE SIXTH JOURNEY THROUGH TIME

VOYAGERS ON THE SIXTH JOURNEY THROUGH TIME

Geronimo Stilton

My name is Stilton, *Geronimo Stilton.*
**I am the editor and publisher
of** *The Rodent's Gazette,* **the most
famouse newspaper on Mouse Island.
I'm about to tell you the story of one
of my fabumouse adventures! But
first, let me introduce the other mice
in this story . . .**

Thea Stilton

**My sister, Thea, is athletic and brave!
She's also a special correspondent
for** *The Rodent's Gazette.*

TRAP

**My cousin Trap is a terrible
prankster sometimes! His favorite
hobby is playing jokes on me . . . but
he's family, and I love him!**

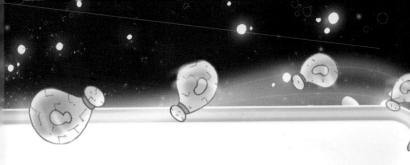

Benjamin

Benjamin is my favorite little nephew. He's a sweet and caring ratlet, and he makes me so proud!

Bugsy Wugsy

Bugsy is Benjamin's best friend. She's a cheerful and lively rodent — sometimes too lively! But she's like family to us!

Professor Paws von Volt

Professor von Volt is a genius inventor who has dedicated his life to making amazing new discoveries. His latest invention is the Cheese-O-Sphere, a new kind of time machine that's causing all sorts of trouble!

My A.A.A.A.

My story starts on a Saturday afternoon in autumn. Holey cheese, it was one of those afternoons that make you want to *curl up* with a good book!

The wind was roaring outside, and freezing rain was tapping on the windows.

PLINK! PLINK! PLINK! PLINK!

But me? I was fabumousely happy. This was the ideal afternoon to enact my **A.A.A.A.**: my Amazing Agenda for an AWESOME AFTERNOON!

Are you wondering what that is?

I'll explain, but first, let me introduce myself. My name is Stilton, *Geronimo Stilton*. I run *The Rodent's Gazette*, the most famouse newspaper on Mouse Island!

Now that you know who I am, maybe you've already guessed what my **A.A.A.A.** is? It has four steps:

1. Laaaaze aaaaround until laaaate!
2. Have an aaaafternoon snaaaack of aaaaged Aaaasiago!
3. Relaaaax in my paaaawchair (in front of my faaaavorite TV show)!
4. Get some aaaair in the paaaark!

Now I was on step three of my **A.A.A.A.** I had just settled into my favorite pawchair with my slippers, and I was about to watch my favorite

show (Mice Throughout History) when the doorbell rang.

It was my cousin Trap. He ran through my door like a tornado, yelling, "**Make waaady!**" Cheese and crackers, what a racket!

Then he grabbed the remote control and plopped down in my chair. But first, he stuck a DVD in the player, yelling, "Get a load of this, Cousin! Quit watching those boring shows of yours!"

I tried to **PROTEST**. "B-but I a-actually really wanted to see *Mice Throughout History*. In this episode, they're squeaking about the Trojan War and —"

Trap **flicked** my ear. "See? I told you! You're older than a dinosaur, dustier than a mummy, and more boring than a moldy cheese wrapper! The Trojan War? That's old stuff. It's all behind us! Boring!"

Then he launched forward. Before I could stop him, he ripped the antenna off my TV. **Squeak!**

"There!" he exclaimed, satisfied. "I did that for your own good. You'll thank me later! This movie I brought will give you a real **shock**."

I shook my snout. I didn't like the sound of that! "What kind of movie is this?"

"It's **marvemouse**, Gerrykins! It's called *Jurassic Terror 2: The Return of T. rex*. It's all about hungry **DINOSAURS** in search of fresh meat!"

Now, if you know me, you know that I am a bit of a 'fraidy mouse. **Scary movies** make my fur stand on end!

Before I could say anything, the doorbell rang again. Whew! This time, it was my nephew Benjamin and his friend Bugsy Wugsy.

Benjamin threw his arms around my neck and yelled, "Surprise!"

Bugsy scampered into my house and bolted to the TV, squeaking, "Hoorraaaay! Jurassic Terror 2!"

Benjamin gave me a high five. "Wow! Cool,

Surprise!

Hi, Uncle G!

Uncle — I didn't think you were so BRAVE! Can we stay and watch the movie with you?"

I didn't want to look like a scaredy-mouse, so I said, "Umm, of course! But if there are scenes that are too scary, make sure you close your EYES! Don't worry, I'm right here."

Trap snickered. "I think you're the only one here who's scared, Germeister!"

Trying to look brave, I started the movie.

Squeak! What a Jurassic fright!

How Jurassically scary!

Yum! Cool! Wow!

THE SMELL OF BAD NEWS!

My teeth were chattering in fear, and I held my paws over my eyes during the SCARY SCENES. Unfortunately, I had **no trouble** hearing the growls and grunts of the starving T. rexes!

Just then my doorbell rang for the third time that day.

Ding dong!

I hurried to open the door — anything to get away from that movie! — and found the **mailmouse** standing outside.

Telegram!

He squeaked, "TELEGRAAAAAAAM! Urgent telegram for Mr. Stilton!"

"That's me!" I said quickly.

I tried to take the telegram from his paw . . . but the mailmouse wouldn't let go!

"Mr. Stilton, are you SURE you want to read this telegram?" he asked. "I think it smells like bad news! I have a fabumouse nose — I know what I'm talking about."

My whiskers were trembling. Was this envelope full of trouble?

MAYBE the mailmouse was right . . .

Are you sure you want to read this?

Well, maybe . . . maybe not . . .

MAYBE it was better not to know!

Then it struck me. Someone might have sent this telegram because they needed my *HELP*! I took a deep breath and said, "Yes, I want to read it. It's urgent — paw it over!"

The mailmouse peered at me over his **glasses**. "Are you sure? Totally, completely sure? I've seen many mice faint over a telegram. I know about bad news. I don't think you want to know what this says!"

I squeaked at the top of my lungs, exasperated, "I do — I'm sure!"

I don't think you want to know!

Paw it over!

I pulled the telegram one way . . .
The mailmouse pulled it the other way . . .

. . . until the envelope ripped!

I fell backward and **hit** my head on the ground.

THUNK!

The last thing I heard was the mailmouse saying, "I told him he shouldn't have anything to do with that telegram!"

When I woke up, I was lying on my couch. There was a bag of ice on the **enormouse** bump on my head.

I told him so!

Argh!

"Cheesy cream puffs — ouch!" I muttered.

Thea appeared next to me and gave me a huge hug. "You really **SCARED** me!" she squeaked. "How is it possible that you seem to hit your head **EVERYWHERE**?"

I shrugged. "It's not my fault! It was the telegram . . . I mean, the mailmouse . . . I mean, the envelope!"

Trap giggled. "Oh, calm down, Thea. Geronimo has a hard head!"

Benjamin ran over to **hug** me, without squeaking a word. Bugsy, on the other paw, began yelling in my ear about all the times she had gotten bumps and bruises. Thundering cattails, that mouse could talk!

Only then did I notice that I still had the **RIPPED** envelope in my paw. "Here, Thea,

you read it," I muttered. "I'm more terrified than a rat with a cat on his tail! Who knows what it might say!"

Thea put the **pieces** of the telegram together and read it out loud . . .

14

TELEGRAM

New Mouse City
Post Office
Mouse Island

Geronimo Stilton
8 Mouseford Lane
New Mouse City,
Mouse Island 13131

DEAR GERONIMO – STOP
THIS IS AN EMERGENCY – STOP
A JURASSIC EMERGENCY – STOP
BE READY TO LEAVE AT ONCE – STOP
I SAID AT ONCE – STOP
I MEAN NOW – STOP
I MEAN IMMEDIATELY – STOP
LEAVE THIS MINUTE – STOP
HURRY – STOP
WHY HAVEN'T YOU LEFT – STOP
SIGNED PROF VON VOLT

WHOOOOOSH!

Holey cheese balls, the telegram was a **_super-urgent_** message from my friend Professor von Volt! I had to get my tail in gear. What if the professor was in danger?

Even though the big bump on my head was throbbing, I jumped to my paws and shouted, "Shake a tail! Everyone out! Professor von Volt needs us!"

We **darted** outside, but there was nobody around.

We looked to the right: nobody!

We looked to the left: nobody!

We looked up: nobody!

The street was totally DESERTED.

STRANGE!

But the telegram had said to leave at once . . .

Suddenly, we heard a voice.
"YOU'RE LATE!"

Then something sucked us up like a giant vacuum cleaner!
HOLEY CHEEEEEEEEEESE!

Whoaaaa!

Ohhh!

WHOOOOSH!

There's nobody here!

A moment later, we found ourselves inside Professor von Volt's **Incredible Airship** — his supersecret flying laboratory!

The professor was twisting his tail in knots. "Geronimo, I've been waiting for you! What took so long?"

I patted him on the shoulder. "I'm sorry, Professor! It's all the **mailmouse's** fault, I mean the telegram's fault, I mean the bump's fault! I fainted, and —"

The professor hugged me. "It doesn't matter,

Where are we?

Incredible!

Professor!

I was waiting for you!

Geronimo. Thank you for coming! I knew I could count on *you and your family*!"

Then he added proudly, "By the way, Geronimo, did you like the **guest vacuum**? And the INVISIBILITY PAINT? The paint is new. It makes the airship invisible!"

I grinned. "It's incredible, Professor!"

Trap elbowed me. "Of course it's incredible, you cheesebrain! That's why he calls it the **Incredible Airship**!"

"Now follow me," Professor von Volt said, "and I'll tell you why I asked you to come so **quickly**. But first, put these on . . ."

He pawed over some super-reinforced rubber **clothes**. I had a bad feeling about this!

Then he added, "On our way to the

THE INCREDIBLE AIRSHIP!

1. Professor von Volt's room
2. Guest room
3. Guest room
4. Sauna
5. Thermal pools
6. Pantry
7. Game room
8. Library
9. Café
10. Conference room
11. Living/Recovery room
12. Changing room
13. Bee room
14. Dining room
15. Kitchen
16. Storage room
17. Command room
18. Motor room with invisibility paint machine
19. Laboratory with vacuum-everything system
20. Meeting room

We won't tell you where the supersecret room is . . . what kind of secret would it be if we did?

SECRET room, I'll show you the latest additions to my laboratory!"

Cheese niblets, the airship really was incredible! We visited the **COMMAND ROOM**, the LABORATORY, the `library`, and even the THERMAL POOLS and the SAUNA.

The professor had perfected his **SECRET** laboratory since the last journey through time. Now it was even more modern, ecological, and super-equipped!

As we walked AROUND the laboratory, I couldn't help wondering why the professor had

Follow me!

made us put on those super-reinforced, super-lined rubber suits.

For the love of cheese, it was definitely strange! We all looked like rubber dolls. How ridiculous!

Finally, we arrived at a room with an armored door like the ones in a bank vault. Above the door were warning signs, advising us to KEEP OUT.

My whiskers were wobbling. What was in that room?

Unfortunately, I was about to find out!

DANGER!
KEEP OUT!

CHOMP! CHOMP! CHOMP!

Professor von Volt entered a combination on the door. The complicated lock sprung open. **Click!**

Then the armed door swung open. I was scared out of my fur!

The professor turned and whispered, "Shhhhh, stay quiet! It's dark because *he* is SLEEPING."

I asked, "Huh? Who?"

But the professor held a paw to his lips and tiptoed into the **SUPERSECRET ROOM.** It was dark inside!

Suddenly, something **BIT** my tail! Squeeeeeeak!

Chomp! Chomp!

Rotten rat's teeth — ouch!

When the professor **finally**

Ouch!

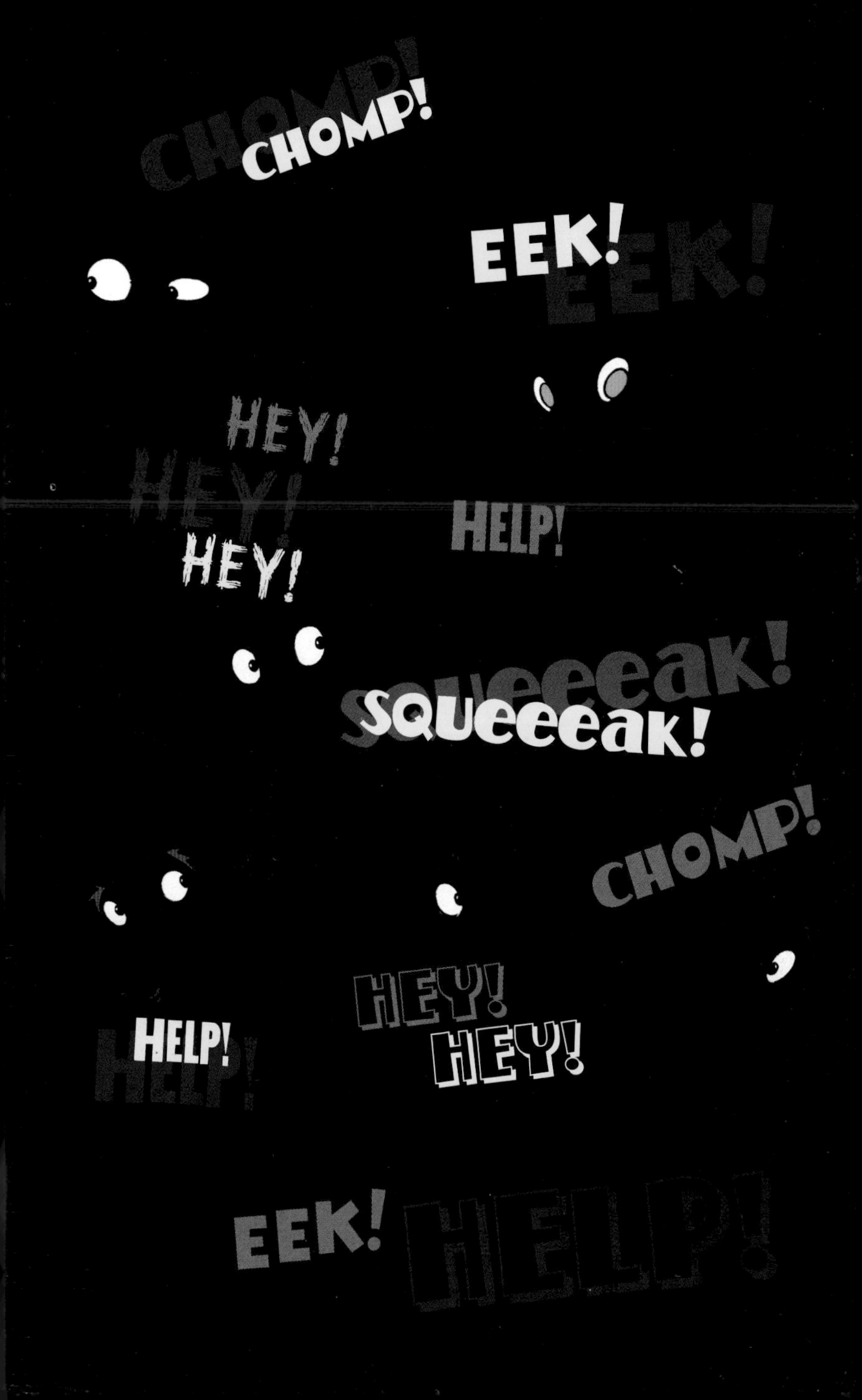
CHOMP!
EEK!
HEY!
HEY!
HEY!
HELP!
SQUEEEAK!
CHOMP!
HEY!
HEY!
HELP!
EEK!
HELP!

turned on the lights, I was squeakless. There was a baby **Triceratops** standing in front of me!

Benjamin yelled, "Hey, that's . . . Tops!"

Holey cheese, Benjamin was right!

It really was **TOPS**. I had met him on my first journey through time!

He seemed to recognize me, too, because he **JUMPED** into my arms and cheerfully bit my snout!

Chomp!

"Hey, what's this little guy doing here?" I asked.

The professor explained. "Well, when I told you there was a JURASSIC EMERGENCY, I really meant a Cretaceous one! That's the period Tops comes from, remember, Geronimo?"

He pulled back a sheet and showed us an enormouse crystal shaped like a cheese ball. It had mathematical formulas and electronic circuits on it. "This is the Cheese-O-Sphere!" he said.

Then the professor sighed. "This is my new time machine, but it's also the cause of all my problems. I sent it to the Cretaceous period to test it out, but it returned with a passenger: TOPS!"

"Can we go in?" Benjamin asked.

The professor nodded. "I'll tell you how it works. This is essentially an enormouse crystal made of synthetic silicoswiss, charged with electrocheese from pure Gorgonzolon."

THE CHEESE-O-SPHERE

This is an **enormouse crystal** made of synthetic silicoswiss. It is powered by an electrocheese charge from pure Gorgonzolon and **works like a giant computer**. To make it go, you need to know the secret formula – the **amperat equation**.

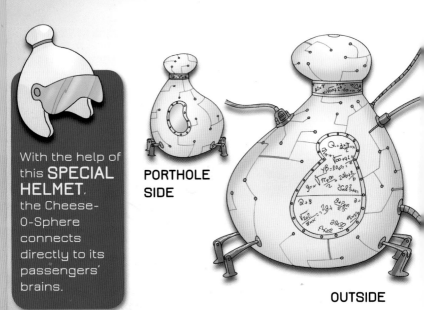

With the help of this **SPECIAL HELMET**, the Cheese-O-Sphere connects directly to its passengers' brains.

PORTHOLE SIDE

OUTSIDE

AMPERAT EQUATION: fsc = Gorg/DeGorg x [Fsc]³
The propulsion speed of the Cheese-O-Sphere is equal to the amount of deGorgonzolized Gorgonzolon multiplied by the fusion speed of the cheese cubed.

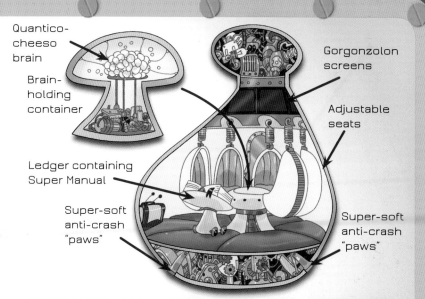

Quantico-cheeso brain

Brain-holding container

Ledger containing Super Manual

Super-soft anti-crash "paws"

Gorgonzolon screens

Adjustable seats

Super-soft anti-crash "paws"

If you carry out the **PROPER PROCEDURE**, travelers will materialize precisely in the predetermined destination, wearing the clothing of that time period and capable of squeaking and understanding the language. Upon arrival, the Cheese-O-Sphere will blend perfectly with its environment.

The machine is simple, but the manual is extremely complicated! It's really a **SUPER MANUAL** because it contains information about all possible historical destinations! It should be read from cover to cover before embarking on a journey. This way, the Cheese-O-Sphere will be guaranteed to sync with the proper time period.

Benjamin exclaimed, "Wow, this is really fabumouse!"

Thea agreed. "What a mousetastic design, Professor!"

"Unfortunately," the Professor explained, "the Cheese-O-Sphere is defective! Once again, I need to ask you to go on a dangerous MISSION and —"

Trap interrupted. "Since I am the most intelligent rodent here, I already understand what you're trying to say. You need us to BRING Tops back home, right?"

Professor von Volt nodded.

Everyone SQUEAKED enthusiastically, except for me!

Rat-munching rattlesnakes, were they crazy? "Well, I would be **HAPPY** to go . . . I mean, I guess . . . I won't let you down, Professor. Won't it be DANGEROUS, though?" I asked.

The professor's snout grew serious. "It won't just be dangerous — it will be super-dangerous! Super-duper-dangerous! Before I send you back to the past, I want to do one more test. I need to make absolutely sure that the machine won't disintegrate during the trip."

Disintegrate? Rancid ricotta!

As Tops **nibbled** at my tail, the professor said, "Get ready! On the count of three, close your eyes and plug your ears!"

He cried, "ONE, TWO, THREE!" Then he pulled the lever.

FIVE INTRUDERS!

There was a big boom, a flash of bright white light — and then the Cheese-O-Sphere disappeared!

"Now we just have to wait," the professor said. "To thoroughly test the machine, I sent it to four different historic periods. Before I allow passengers inside."

Crusty cat litter!

By now I was PALER than a ball of mozzarella during a full moon! I muttered, "Th-th-thanks, P-P-Professor. I d-d-don't want to d-d-disintegrate. *I'm t-t-too fond of my f-f-fur!*"

As we waited, I nibbled at my **paws**.

What would happen?

A few minutes passed, but it felt like a century!

And then . . .

There was another big boom, a flash of bright white light — and then the Cheese-O-Sphere reappeared!

The door opened with a hiss.

HISSSSSSSSSSSS!

A Parmesan-colored cloud appeared.

PFFFFFFFFFFFFT!

Then four mice stepped out of the machine.
Squeak!

First there was a rodent with long blond hair, dressed like someone from ancient Greece.

She looked around, batting her long EYE/aShES, and asked, "Oh, where am I? And where are my maids? And all the WARRiORS? Why aren't I in Troy?"

Then I recognized her. This was *Helen of Troy*, the most beautiful mouse of all time!

Then a **muscular** mouse stepped forward, brandishing a sword. "Who are you? How dare you?" he thundered. "I will destrooooyyyyy you! Where I walk, grass no longer grows!"

I recognized him, too — it was the fearsome **Attila the Hun**!

Then another rodent walked toward us. He looked very serious and had a crown on his head.

Squeak, it was **CHARLEMAGNE**!

Finally, another mouse jumped down. He seemed very intelligent and asked, "Where am I? Did I reach the Indies? Where is my ship?"

Holey cheese! It was the explorer and navigator **Christopher Columbus**!

I'LL TAKE CARE OF YOU, RATS!

Seeing those four mice from the PAST, Professor von Volt fainted. We had to wake him up with mozzarella-scented smelling salts!

Luckily, I always carry a vial in my pocket. I guess you could say that I faint easily!

Meanwhile, chaos erupted in the lab!

Helen complained, "Humph, I have really had

Chomp!

Professor!

Poor mouse!

enough of these mousenappings! My husband, Menelaus, will take care of you rats!"

HELEN OF TROY

Christopher Columbus said, "Messengers, I demand to be taken back to my ship! I need to report to Queen Isabella! She will take care of you rats!"

CHRISTOPHER COLUMBUS

Charlemagne thundered, "How dare you! I am king of the Franks and Holy Roman Emperor! My knights will take care of you rats!"

CHARLEMAGNE

Attila the Hun looked furious. "How dare you capture me? I will take care of you rats myself! I will destrooooyyyy you!"

Tops NIBBLED at my tail, and Benjamin squeaked with

ATTILA THE HUN

excitement. Bugsy shrieked and **tugged** at my arm as I tried to explain. "Excuse me, everyone, there was a **misunderstanding**! We will take you home right away!"

Trap jumped **toward** Attila and Charlemagne and put his arms around their shoulders. "Hey there, **BiG OL' ATTiLA**. Hey, **CHARLEY**, how's it going? Don't listen to that silly cousin of mine! I'm the boss here, and us bosses understand one another, right?"

Before I could say anything, the professor woke up and walked over to me.

He looked as pale as a tub of ricotta. "QUICK, Geronimo! We need to send them all back right away. We risk changing history!"

Then he pawed over two VIALS. The first was full of blue liquid. The other had green liquid inside. "Be careful not to mix them up, Geronimo!" he said seriously. "The blue one is a MEMORY-ERASING ESSENCE. Give a sip to each of our guests right before they return to their time periods! That way, they will forget about their ADVENTURES

outside their own time. This is fabumousely important — otherwise we risk changing history.

"The green liquid is the *brain essence*. You'll need it in order to connect your brain with the Cheese-O-Sphere. You must each drink one **spoonful** during the departure procedure."

I took the **vials** and placed them carefully in my pocket.

Then the professor showed me an **ENORMOUSE** book. "This is the Super Manual. It contains all of the available information about all different time periods. You must read it before **LEAVING**. That way, the Cheese-O-Sphere will sync up with the right time period!"

Then he put a sheet of paper in my paw. "And this is the departure procedure."

Chomp!

What's this?

Here's the Super Manual!

The professor twisted his tail nervously. "I'm warning you, follow the departure procedure precisely! And don't forget the amperat equation. Now it's time for all of you to get aboard the Cheese-O-Sphere — you must leave at once!"

I peered around.

The whole lab was bubbling with confusion and chaos. Holey cheese! How could I convince everyone to get inside the time machine — and fast?

Suddenly, I had a mousetastic idea. "The last one inside the Cheese-O-Sphere is a piece of moldy mozzarella!" I cried.

The last one in is a piece of moldy mozzarella!

Chomp!

Trying to set a good example, I headed toward the Cheese-O-Sphere.

I'm a total clumsypaws, so of course I tripped on my tail. Squeak! Trap passed me, but he was shoved aside by Attila as Bugsy dodged Thea and Benjamin.

Guess who was the last one inside the Cheese-O-Sphere? Me!

Cheesy cream puffs, I was a mouserific mess . . .

But at least I had managed to get everyone into the Cheese-O-Sphere!

WHY DID I always end up looking like such a cheesebrain?

I closed the door, took a deep breath, and announced, "Ladies and gentlemice, it's official: a fabumouse new journey through time is about to begin!"

DESTINATION:

THE CRETACEOUS PERIOD

Do You Want to Go Back Home or Not?

I sealed the door of the Cheese-O-Sphere shut, as Professor von Volt had instructed. Then I held the departure procedure in my paw and addressed the rest of the passengers. "Now we will take you all back home. Who wants to go first?"

Everyone began **yelling** at once.

"Me first! I am a lady!" shouted Helen of Troy.

Me first! Me first! Me first! Me first! Or I'll destrooooy you! Um . . .

"No, me first! Otherwise **I WILL DESTROOOYYYY YOU**!!" Attila thundered.

"Me first, I am the oldest!" grumbled Christopher Columbus.

Charlemagne squeaked up. "Oh no, me first! After all, I am the noblest!"

"Sniiick! Sniiiick!" yelled Tops, and I knew that he was trying to say, "Me first, I'm the youngest!"

Swiss cheese on rye, I didn't know what to do. Who would we take home first?

Luckily, Thea put a stop to all the yelling. "QUIIIIEEEEETTTT!"

Quiiiieeeeetttt!

Everyone fell silent, and Thea took the situation into her own paws. "Ladies and gentlemice, either you do as I say or **NO ONE** goes home, understand?

"First: my brother Geronimo will tell you the rules!

47

"**Second**: you will obey them!"

"**Third**: you will cooperate!"

"**Fourth**: there will be no fighting!"

"**Fifth**: there will be no arguing!"

"**Sixth**: there will be no complaining!"

"**Seventh**: there will be no threats, especially if you have sharp swords! Do you understand me, Attila?"

Rotten rat's teeth, my sister was tough! Even Attila the Hun **looked** at her with admiration.

What a spitfire!

Understand, Attila?

I took advantage of the SILENCE and tried to explain the departure procedure to everyone.

Since I had already completed step one, I moved along to step two. There was no time

Departure Procedure

ATTENTION: THE CHEESE-O-SPHERE WORKS BY SYNCING WITH TRAVELERS' BRAINS. BEFORE DEPARTURE, YOU MUST FOLLOW THIS PROCEDURE PRECISELY — THERE IS NO ROOM FOR ERROR!

1) ENTER THE CHEESE-O-SPHERE AND SEAL THE DOOR SHUT (otherwise, you could get lost in time).

2) TURN THE RED SWITCH TO THE "LISTEN AND LEARN" POSITION (careful: there are thirty-seven different switches to choose from).

3) PUT ON YOUR HELMETS AND READ THE SUPER MANUAL OUT LOUD (make sure to read the information for only the time period you want to travel to — otherwise, you could go to the wrong time).

4) DRINK A SPOONFUL OF THE BRAIN ESSENCE, TO BOOST YOUR BRAIN CAPACITY (it is disgusting, but you need to drink all of it).

5) TURN UPSIDE DOWN SO THE BLOOD WILL RUSH TO YOUR BRAINS (careful not to fall).

6) UTTER THE AMPERAT EQUATION (this must be done flawlessly, otherwise the Cheese-O-Sphere won't leave).
fsc - Gorg/DeGorg x [Fsc]³

The propulsion speed of the Cheese-O-Sphere is equal to the amount of deGorgonzolized Gorgonzolon multiplied by the fusion speed of the cheese cubed.

to waste! I turned the red switch to the "listen and learn" position.

A door opened and an enormouse ear came out, turned itself toward me, and ordered, "Read, Cheesebrain! I'm all ears!"

Trap snickered. "Did you hear that, Gerrykins? Even the Cheese-O-Sphere thinks you're a cheesebrain!"

I rolled my eyes. "All right, Trap, I may be a

cheesebrain sometimes, but that's not important right now. We have a mission to complete!"

I opened the SUPER MANUAL. "Now I will read everything about our first destination: **THE CRETACEOUS PERIOD**!"

Benjamin hugged Tops and squeaked with joy. "Are you happy, Tops? You're going home!"

TOPS nibbled cheerfully at Benjamin's whiskers.

I added, "Before I read, let's **put on** our helmets. It's time for us to sync up to the Cheese-O-Sphere."

Are you happy? You're going home!

Chomp!

The Cretaceous Period and the Dinosaurs

Our planet is very old — about 4.6 billion years old, in fact. To measure the phases of life on our planet, scholars have divided the history of Earth into eras and periods.

The dinosaurs developed in the **MESOZOIC ERA**, which is divided into three periods: **TRIASSIC, JURASSIC**, and **CRETACEOUS**.

The **CRETACEOUS PERIOD** began about 145 million years ago. During this period, Earth began to look more like what we know today.

WATER LILIES

The **CLIMATE** was hot and humid during much of the period. Tropical plants such as palm trees even grew in areas that are cold today, like Alaska!

Perhaps the greatest new development of the period was the appearance of **FLOWERS**! Water lilies and magnolias grew in the forests next to the conifers. It is believed that **INSECTS** like bees and butterflies became widespread, and they carried pollen from flower to flower.

MAGNOLIAS

During the Cretaceous period, many REPTILES similar to our modern-day serpents developed. The ocean was home to large iguanas and sharks. In the swamps and along the rivers, there were BIRDS with webbed feet. And among the mammals, marsupials similar to opossums appeared.

REPTILES

The DINOSAURS, which had first appeared during the Triassic period, developed new means of defense during the CRETACEOUS PERIOD.

TYRANNOSAURUS REX

The HERBIVORES, which ate plants and vegetables, had bodies protected by shells, plates, and horns.

The CARNIVOROUS dinosaurs refined their hunting techniques: their vision improved, their teeth got sharper, their claws became more powerful, and their speed increased significantly.

And possibly the greatest land predator of all time appeared: the terrible TYRANNOSAURUS REX!

GET YOUR CHOMPERS OFF THE SUPER MANUAL!

I was still reading about the Cretaceous period when I heard a strange sound.

Chomp! muuunch! Chomp!

Holey cheese balls, Tops was **EATING** the Super Manual!

Fangs off!

Chomp! Munch! Chomp!

I yelped, "Hey, get your chompers off the Super Manual!"

Bugsy and Benjamin helped me get the book away from Tops, but he had already nibbled on an enormouse chunk of it. What a disaster!

But what could I do? I had to move on to the next step of the departure procedure.

Next was step four: drink a spoonful of the brain essence!

I pulled the two vials out of my pocket. My whiskers began to shake. I couldn't remember — which was the right one?

Was it the green one or the blue one?

The green one or the blue one?

WHAT STRESS!
WHAT STRESS!
WHAT STRESS!

Are you ready?

Trap noticed that I was confused, so he ripped the vial of blue liquid from my paws. "What in the name of cheese would you do if I weren't here to help, Cousin? The boss should take responsibility, and I'm the boss, so . . . I decide!"

Before I could squeak, he plugged my nose and poured a spoonful of blue liquid in my mouth. "Geronimo, you get to be the guinea pig! Someone has to sacrifice himself for science!"

Suddenly, I felt tremendmousely confused . . .

"Wait. What am I doing here? Who am I?"

Trap PINCHED my ear.

"Aha!" Trap cried in triumph. "So the blue one is the MEMORY-ERASING ESSENCE! You see how easy that was to figure out?"

Then he gave everyone a spoonful from the vial of green liquid. It was awful! It tasted like Gorgonzola gone bad, rotten fish, and old socks!

But at least it brought my memory back. Whew!

Next, we all turned upside down and uttered the amperat equation. There was a flash of light — and the Cheese-O-Sphere took off!

Mouse Smoothie!

The Cheese-O-Sphere began to

spin and spin

like a top, shaking us up like mouse **SMOOThies**! Then, suddenly,

THERE WAS A BIG BOOM . . .

A FLASH OF BRIGHT LIGHT . . .

And finally the Cheese-O-Sphere stopped.

The door hissed open. HISSSSSSSSSSS!

I could see a mozzarella-colored cloud. PFFFFFFFFFFFT!

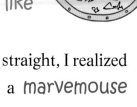

We all stumbled out of the time machine.

My head was spinning like crazy.

When I was finally able to see straight, I realized that we were standing before a marvemouse prehistoric landscape.

We had finally arrived at our destination: the **CRETACEOUS PERIOD**!

"Mouserific!" I squeaked.

Well, almost...

I tried to squeak — but a powerful roar came out of my mouth instead!

"RRRRROOOOAAAARRR!"

Fossilized feta, what had happened? A **moment** later, I suddenly understood. I

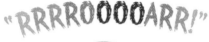

looked at my travel companions and realized that they were **disguised** as dinosaurs, too!

I couldn't help squeaking, "Heeeeelp!"

But instead, I roared!

The others roared, too, but I understood exactly what they were saying. Bones and stones, we were all speaking the dinosaur language!

Then I remembered what Professor von Volt had said: we would arrive in each time period already in disguise and able to **SPEAK** the language. But I never would have imagined being disguised as dinosaurs!

This new **TIME MACHINE** really was mousetastic!

HERBIVORES OR CARNIVORES?

Attila growled in his dinosaur voice, "I will destrooooy you!"

CHARLEMAGNE yelled, "I've landed amongst the dragons! Never fear, I will take them all out!" When he reached for his sword, he realized that he had **dinosaur paws**! "Oh! I'm a dragon, too!" he roared in alarm. "What kind of DARK MAGIC is this?"

I explained that it was not magic, it was science. We had gone back in time to the prehistoric era, when the land was populated by **dinosaurs**!

It's not magic!

Attila, **CHARLEMAGNE**, *Helen of Troy,* and even Christopher Columbus only believed me when I took my dinosaur head off.

Thea explained, "It's like a play — we're just wearing costumes!"

Trap smirked. "Yeah, and you really should keep those **masks** on if you want to stay alive, got it? There are **ENORMOUSE** beasts around here who love fresh mouse meat."

"Some dinosaurs are herbivores, though," Benjamin put in.

I felt my fur growing pale. "That's true . . . the problem is recognizing which ones are carnivores before they eat you for a snack!"

Bugsy grinned. "Don't worry! I'm a dinosaur expert. I know all of the different types of dinosaurs by heart — we studied them in school! I can tell you if they are herbivores or carnivores."

"Everyone listen up, I'm the boss!" Trap said.

Dinosaurs of the Cretaceous Period

Herbivore

CONFUCIUSORNIS
One of the oldest creatures on record that had a beak similar to the beaks of modern-day birds.

Herbivore

PROTOCERATOPS
Adults were about 6 feet long and weighed over 400 pounds.

Herbivore

CORYTHOSAURUS
Had a bony crest on top of its head. Its nostrils rose up through the crest, possibly giving it a better sense of smell.

Herbivore

IGUANODON
A mobile lower jaw allowed these dinosaurs to chew and eat large quantities of tough plants, like ferns.

Carnivore

PTERANODON
Possibly ate fish that it caught by gliding its pointy beak across the surface of the water while flying.

Carnivore

TYRANNOSAURUS REX
One of the biggest carnivores ever to exist on Earth! It was also fast, possibly running at speeds from 10 to 25 miles per hour.

Omnivore

OVIRAPTOR
Was an omnivore, which means it ate a combination of animals and plants.

Carnivore

VELOCIRAPTOR
Was even faster than the T. rex, possibly reaching speeds of almost 40 miles per hour!

"If Bugsy says 'herbivore,' you stay put. But if she says '**CARNIVORE**,' you run as fast as your paws will take you! Is that clear?"

Clear or not, we didn't have time for more explanations. Tops suddenly bolted away at a gallop, yelling, "**Sniiiiiiiick!**"

This time, I understood that he had said, "Home!" A moment later, Tops had disappeared into the PREHISTORIC FOREST.

Cheese niblets! **TOPS** was just a baby. I couldn't let him run off on his own!

I'm exhausted!

I'm the boss!

No, I am!

He could get LOST, or run into a big, ferocious dinosaur — like a T. rex!

POOR TOPS! I may be a 'fraidy mouse, but I couldn't let anything bad happen to him.

So I made a fast decision. "Quick, let's follow him — we're a team! Mice for one, mice for all!"

Charlemagne and Attila pushed to the front of the group, yelling, "I am the boss, follow me!"

I let them pass. I didn't care who was in command. I only **cared** that Tops made it home safe and sound.

Quick, follow me!

Sniiick!

Okay, fine, I had a soft spot for that little guy . . . even though he had a bad habit of biting my tail!

Benjamin and Bugsy raced off like mice on a cheese hunt. After all, Tops was their good friend! The rest of us followed, while Helen complained, "I'm sure to **break** a pawnail on all these rocks! And this humid weather is going to frizz my fur! Do you know how long it took my maids to get it looking like this?"

I'm going to break a pawnail!

We ran and ran and ran, following **TOPS'S** pawprints for hours. WHeW!

We headed deeper into the **wild** prehistoric landscape, amid enormouse ferns, giant monkey puzzles*, and super-stinky **swamps**! But there was still no sign of Tops.

Where could he have gone?

* Monkey puzzles were conifer trees native to parts of the Southern Hemisphere.

That way!

Let's follow the tracks!

THERE'S BEEN A MISUNDERSTANDING!

A moment later, I breathed a sigh of relief.

A small, familiar snout popped out of a nearby group of triceratops. **IT WAS TOPS!** He ran up and began to rub his head on us.

We **hugged** him happily.

Sniiiick!

Tops!

He thanked us, and we understood his words. "Thanks, friends. It was good to see you again, but it's even better to be back home!"

I was **happy** for the little guy.

I couldn't help thinking about our first journey through time, when we had found an ABANDONED egg — and then Tops had hatched out of it! At first, he had mistaken us for his family, but eventually Tops found a group of TRICERATOPS that became his family. Just thinking about it warmed my heart like melted cheese.

Sniiick!

We were still exchanging hugs when I found myself snout-to-snout with two enormouse **TRICERATOPS**. Rancid ricotta!

They stared at me threateningly, flaring their nostrils and scratching the ground with their paws.

GRRR! GRRRRRR! GRRRRRR!

"Who are you? What are you doing here? What do you want?"

"Get your paws off our little one!"

Grrr!
Grrrrrr!
Grrrrrrrrrr!

"**Moldy mozzarella**," I muttered. "This doesn't look good . . ." Then I tried to explain. "Um, there's been a misunderstanding!"

Just then, Tops noticed what was going on. "Mom, Dad, these are my friends!"

But the male triceratops **growled**, "We told you not to talk to strangers, son. These creatures are not triceratops!"

Tops's mother muttered, "I don't even know **WHAT** they are. I've never seen dinosaurs like these."

His dad added, "And they **stink**! They stink like mice. I don't trust them!"

I had to say something. "Of course we smell like mice — we *are* mice! We come from very far away, and we don't want to hurt your little one. We're his friends!"

"**It's true, they saved me!**" Tops piped up.

Tops's dad thundered, "Well . . . you might be

friendly . . . and you may have even **SAVED**
Tops . . . but I've never **SEEN** you around
these parts before!"

He paused and looked us up and down. "So
let's do this: first we'll charge at you, then we'll
STOMP on you, and then we'll CRUSH
you. If it turns out you really were harmless, oh
well!"

Holey cheese, we were going to be mousemeat!

Then he ordered, *"TRICERATOPS,*
CHARRRRRRGE!"

I stepped in front of Benjamin and Bugsy to
protect them, squeaking, "Wh-wh-who do you

th-th-think you are? Fontina face! Coconut h-h-head! You subspecies of lazy lizard! Bring it on, if you're brave enough!"

Attila hollered at me. "Stop your squeaking and run, rat! You're not SCARING anyone. I know a little something about scaring — you need to try harder!" He puffed up his chest, boasting, "Look and learn! I am an expert! Did you know that my tribe says that

Rooooarrr!

Roooooaaarrr!

where I step, grass no longer grows?"

Then Attila let out a truly terrifying growl. "RRRRROOOOAAAARRR!"

The triceratops all yelled in fear. Then they turned around and ran off as fast as their paws would carry them, making the earth rumble like an **earthquake**!

I was squeakless.

Attila looked awfully proud of himself. "Did

Eek!

you see that, rat? I **TERRORIZED** them!"

Just then, Thea grabbed my paw and squeaked, "Geronimo, look behind us!"

As I turned, I suddenly understood. Attila hadn't made the triceratops run off. What had made them *run* was an angry T. rex, who had just stomped up behind us! Holey rolling boulders, what a mess!

Columbus tapped me on the shoulder.

"Umm, sir? I don't quite understand. Is this tyrannowhatsis an herbivore or a **CARNIVORE**?"

Bugsy responded for me. "Carnivooooore!"

"And he seems **VERY**, **VERY**, **VERY** hungry, and in search of fresh meat! ***run!***" I cried.

We all got our tails in gear and began to ***run*** toward the Cheese-O-Sphere. The T. rex stayed right on our tails, trying to catch us with his giant fangs!

CHOMP!
CHOMP!
ROOOOOOARRR!

YOU HAVE SOME NICE WHISKERS!

We managed to reach the Cheese-O-Sphere just as the T. rex lunged for my tail! Squeak, what a feline fright!

Holey cheese, this time I really did make it by a whisker!

I sealed the door. Then I fainted.

When I came to, I noticed that I no longer had

I'm fainting!

my dinosaur costume on. All I could see were some charming **BIG BLUE EYES** watching me.

It was Helen of Troy! She was waving a linen pawkerchief at me as she WHiSPeReD sweetly, "Poor Geronimo, you're not much of a musclemouse! But you have some nice whiskers. And you do have an **INTELLECTUAL** air about you . . ."

Trap popped into my line of vision. "Oh, *Helen*, don't worry about that cheesebrain. He faints easily! Not like me — I'm courageous, kind, athletic, and I am also the boss! I am most

You're not much of a musclemouse!

Ouch!

definitely worthy of you, a rodent of great class!"

Attila had to squeak up. "No, the toughest, most fascinating, and strongest mouse is . . . **me**!"

"Who do you think you are?" Charlemagne cried. "I'm the **EMPEROR**! The most important rodent of all! Don't listen to them, my sweet Helen . . ."

Even Christopher Columbus got in on the argument. "Well, I am the `most intellectual` of everyone here — and also the most fearless!"

Thundering cattails! I held up my paws for silence.

I didn't want to FIGHT with my cousin, or with anyone else. It was time to take the beautiful

And I am the most important!

And I am the most intellectual!

87

Helen of Troy home. Without wasting time, I began the complicated departure procedure. As I did, I glanced out the porthole, sighing.

I hadn't gotten to say good-bye to **TOPS**!

At that moment, Benjamin yelled, "Uncle G, look!"

I looked, and squeaked with joy. Tops was standing outside the **Cheese-O-Sphere**. He had come to say good-bye to us!

Sniick! Sniick!

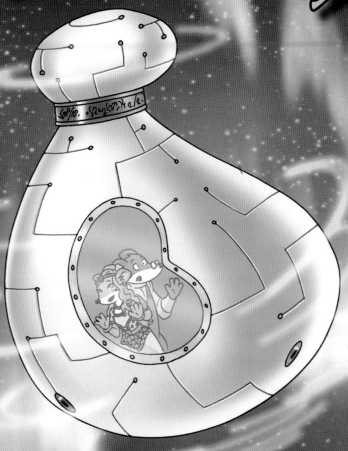

HOLEY CHEESE BALLS!

While I was repeating the departure procedure for the second time, I made a mental note to tell Professor von Volt to simplify it when we got home. Holey cheese balls, it was so complicated!

We put on our helmets. Thundering cattails, we looked so ridiculous!

My helmet was too tight, and I immediately got an enormouse headache. And when Bugsy began to read the information about the Trojan War, Helen interrupted her constantly, squeaking, "It's really incredible! That thing there — what do you call it? A book? — talks about me! But how is that possible?

"I didn't know I had become so famouse!" Helen squeaked.

Argh!

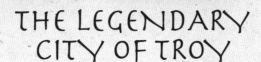

THE LEGENDARY CITY OF TROY

The legendary city of TROY is almost universally accepted to be located in modern-day Turkey. At the time of the TROJAN WAR described in Homer's Iliad (13th century BC), it was of great strategic importance. Given its position at the southern entrance to the Dardanelles, it could control traffic between the Black Sea and Aegean Sea, as well as significant land routes.

GREECE DURING THE TIME OF THE TROJAN WAR

Black Sea

Dardanelles Strait

Troy

Thebes
Corinth
Athens
Mycenae
Argos

Ithaca
Cephalonia
Zakynthos

Pylos

Miletus

Rhodes

Knossos

Crete

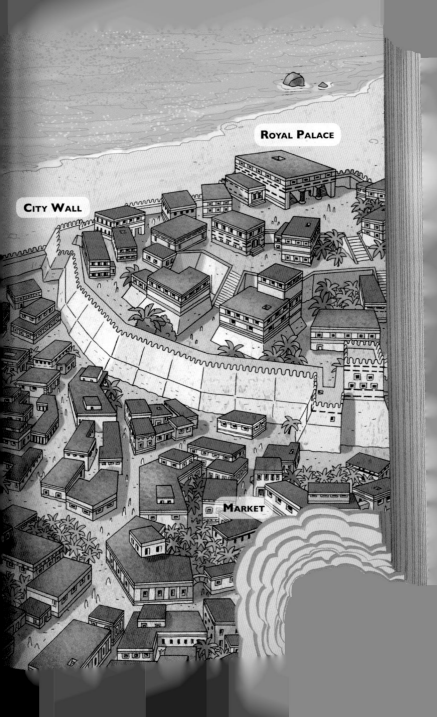

All Because of a GOLDEN APPLE!

According to HOMER'S ILIAD, the story of Troy and the famouse war that destroyed it began in a mythical time when the world was governed by the Greek gods!

By one account, ERIS, the goddess of discord, was not invited to the marriage banquet of Peleus and Thetis (Achilles's parents). When she was turned away at the door, she threw a golden apple on the banquet table that said *To the fairest* on it. BUT WHO WAS THE FAIREST?

A fight immediately broke out between HERA, the powerful wife of Zeus, the king of the gods; ATHENA, the goddess of wisdom; and APHRODITE, the goddess of love.

None of the gods knew how to choose, so Zeus entrusted the task to PARIS, one of the sons of Priam, the king of Troy.

ERIS, THE GODDESS OF DISCORD

HELEN OF TROY

HERA assured him RICHES, ATHENA offered him WISDOM, and APHRODITE promised him the most BEAUTIFUL woman in the world, Helen, wife of Menelaus, the king of Sparta.

Paris unwisely gave the apple to APHRODITE. According to Homer, when he met HELEN, he fell in love with her and brought her with him to Troy.

This enraged Helen's husband, Menelaus. With the help of his brother, Agamemnon, the king of Mycenae, he gathered the Greeks into a great army that would attack Troy.

THE WAR HAD BEGUN!

HOMER The ancient people attribute the *Iliad* and the *Odyssey* (two famous ancient poems) to a poet named Homer. No one knows for sure if he really existed.

Thea said, "Yes, you're famouse — *super-duper famouse!* It is often said that you were the most beautiful rodent of all time! By the way, would you mind answering a few **questions**? The lady rodents of New Mouse City would be thrilled to learn more about you, I'm sure."

Thea pulled out a NOTEBOOK and began to take notes. "Tell me, my dear, what is a day in your *life* like?"

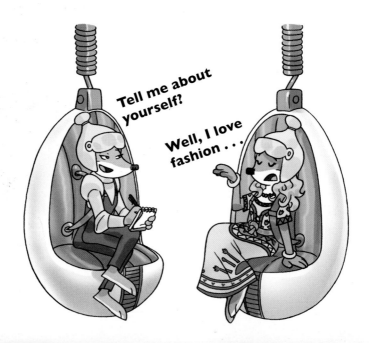

I put up my paws in protest. "Thea, does this seem like the right time for an interview? We need to finish our mission and take *Helen* home!"

Thea gave me a look. "It's always the right time for an interview! You should know that, Geronimo. It's one of the key principles of journalism!"

Helen and Thea chatted about Helen's life while Bugsy continued to read the SUPER MANUAL aloud. Everyone else was busy arguing about who was the biggest, the strongest, and the most important!

For the love of cheese, they were making my brain buzz!

Suddenly, Bugsy interrupted. "Uh-oh . . . I can't read anymore. Tops ate the rest of the pages!"

Tops ate the pages!

"Oh no! What a mousetastic

mess!" I squeaked, my whiskers **wobbling**.

Would the **Cheese-O-Sphere** be able to get us to the right place now?

Would the **PROCEDURE** work?

There was only one way to find out! I had to cross my fingers, **finish** the procedure, and hope! I gave everyone a spoonful of the brain essence, and we turned **upsiDe DoWn** and said the amperat equation together.

There was a flash of light, and the Cheese-O-Sphere took off. It began to spin faster and faster, shaking us up like mouse smoothies!

THERE WAS A GREAT BOOM . . . *A FLASH OF BRIGHT LIGHT* . . . then the Cheese-O-Sphere stopped and the door opened with a hiss.

Before we got off, I gave Helen a spoonful of the

MEMORY-ERASING ESSENCE. That way, she wouldn't remember her adventure through time.

Benjamin looked at me, concerned. "Uncle G, you look pale. Do you feel all right?"

"**I'm great!**" I responded.

But really, I wasn't great, or even good. I felt like I was going to faint from fright!

From what I could remember, Helen of Troy's time was **VERY, VERY, VERY** dangerous!

Who knew what was waiting for us out there?

Battles between fierce, enormouse armies?

Duels to the last whisker between **HEROES** as big as tanks?

Terrifying mythical monsters?

Squeeeak, what an epic* fright!

---

* An epic is a long narrative poem that tells the tale of legendary heroes. Today, it can also mean "grand" or "impressive."

EVEN YOUR WHISKERS ARE TREMBLING!

Trap nudged me with his elbow. "Cousin, don't deny it — you're epically **AFRAID**!"

Attila peered at me. "Rat, everyone can tell that you're **TERRIFIED**! You're as pale as a slab of mozzarella, and even your whiskers are trembling."

I shook my snout. "I'm not afraid!"

OFFENDED, I stepped out of the Cheese-O-Sphere, with my friends right behind me.

Once I got outside, I realized that we all were wearing long, multicolored **CLOTHING**, precious jewels, and wigs with elaborate hairdos, decorated with ribbons and **flowers**! Swiss cheese on rye — we were all wearing dresses!

I scratched my head. My **BRAIN** began to work overtime until I finally understood. The

Cheese-O-Sphere hadn't gotten all the information from the SUPER MANUAL, since Tops had chewed it up. So it had picked up Thea and Helen's conversation about *fashion*.

That's why we were all wearing **dresses**!

All of a sudden, we were surrounded by a crowd of shouting lady rodents!

"*Princess Helen*, Your Majesty! There you are, finally!"

"We found you — what a relief!"

FASHION IN ANCIENT TROY

There are no precise testimonies about FASHION during the time of ancient Troy, but it is thought that the fashions were very similar to the nearby Cretan-Mycenaean civilization.

The RICHEST women may have worn tight-fitting bustiers and flounced skirts.

Trap and the rest of my friends wore typical women's work garments.

Attila was wearing a long dress made of rough linen . . . very chic!

The leather belt highlighted Columbus's waist!

What kind of outfit is this?

Hee, hee!

Grrr . . .

I wore an elegant wig with blond curls to mimic the Trojans' elaborate hairstyles. I have to admit, it really looked good on me!

The colors of these fabrics are very vibrant!

The MEN'S CLOTHING of ancient Troy was likely very simple: men were almost always bare-chested and wore a rigid, short skirt that was open on the sides.

To protect themselves from the cold, they wore cloaks and rectangular capes made of heavy wool and fur during the winter.

This soldier's helmet is made of decorated metal adorned with large feathers.

Here is King Priam, wearing an elegant garment adorned with precious jewels.

Here's Helen in a typical noblewoman's dress.

Children wore tunics with hemmed seams.

The typical men's skirt.

At that point, we had to stay in our female disguises, or they would have found us out!

Helen exclaimed, "Oh, my head hurts!"

I ran to help her, and she looked up at me in confusion. She didn't recognize me after taking the memory-erasing essence.

"I don't remember you, maid. What is your name?" she said slowly.

"Um, I am Geronache," I responded, thinking **QUICKLY**, "and these are my seven sisters: Thea, Bugsy, Benjamandra, Attilina, Charla, Trappuba, and Christofa."

There you are!

Princess Helen!

Your Majesty!

Just then, another *maid* approached and pulled me away from Helen, giving me an **icy** glare. Then she turned to Helen and said sweetly, "Let me take you to your quarters, Your Majesty. The sun is high: it could damage your fur. I am still your favorite, right?"

She gave me a **NASTY LOOK** and then added, whispering, "That Geronache sure is strange! Her hair is such a mess, her dress is wrinkled, and what are those things on her snout?"

Helen waved her paw. "Well, she seems **nice to me**. She must be new — I don't remember her or her sisters."

Then she turned to me. "Geronache, can you tell **stories**? I really like stories!"

WHAT ARE THESE?

MESSY HAIR

WRINKLED DRESS

GERONACHE!

Benjamin answered, "Geronimo — I mean, Geronache is excellent at telling stories!"

"Geronache, I name you the **Royal Storyteller!**" Helen squeaked, clapping her paws. "Follow me, and bring your sisters, too!"

I tried to refuse. "Your Majesty, my **STORIES** are nothing special, nothing like the stories of Homer . . ."

"Homer? Who is this Homer?"

"Well, he's a very famous poet," I explained. "I know some parts of his poems that are precisely about the **TROJAN WAR** . . ."

"War? What war?" Helen said. "There's no war here!"

Trap jumped in. "For now — but if I were you, I would prepare. It doesn't **LOOK GREAT** for you, you know?"

The wicked maid raised her eyebrows. "Oh no! Are you a prophetess, like Cassandra? She also babbles on about wars and calamity . . ."

Helen shrugged. "Well, I don't know anything about war, but tonight you will **perform** at my banquet — that's an order! My Paris and I adore stories!"

I blushed. "Your Majesty, I am a TIMID rodent, and —"

The wicked maid snickered. "Come on, Geronache, you wouldn't want to upset the princess, right?"

Tonight, you will sing for me!

But I . . .

Ha, ha, ha!

PRICKLIER THAN A PORCUPINE!

The maid smirked and whispered in my ear, "You are going to stink tonight! You will be thrown out of the palace and I will never have to see your snout again, or my name isn't Astyanassa!"

Slimy Swiss balls, that Astyanassa was **nastier** than gum in your whiskers!

GUM IN YOUR WHISKERS

Ack!

SIP OF VINEGAR

Gulp!

PRICKLY PORCUPINE

Aaaaahhh!

More SOUP than a sip of vinegar!

And PRICKLIER than a porcupine!

Because of her, I was up to my snout in serious trouble!

"Your Majesty, please let my sister RETIRE to her room. She will need time to prepare for her performance," Thea said.

Helen agreed. "Of course! I will have my guards accompany you to the PALACE, just in case you get the idea to run. I'm warning you, do not embarrass me! Everyone will be there tonight — my beloved Paris; his father, Priam; and the LEGENDARY HECTOR*, our ultimate hero. You have certainly heard of him, right? He is my dear Paris's older brother."

I stuttered, *"O-of course, Your Majesty! I will do my best!"*

Thea grabbed my dress and dragged me to

---

* Hector, the oldest son of Priam and Hecuba, is a Trojan hero. He is the strongest defender of the city, according to Homer's epic poem the *Iliad*.

the MAIDS' QUARTERS in Priam's palace. Two massive guards escorted us, then planted themselves in front of our door. "Do not leave that room," they instructed. "If Her Majesty doesn't have fun tonight, we will turn you into **MOUSE KEBABS**!"

Double-twisted rattails! **NO PRESSURE.**

As soon as we were inside the room, Thea turned to me. "Geronimo, you really are a cheesebrain! Didn't I tell you to leave the talking to me? Now we're stuck here and we can't leave on our mission."

Trap smirked. "Geronimo is the world champion of trouble."

Holey cheese, this was a **fur-raising** situation for sure!

Then Benjamin and Bugsy took my paws. "Have courage, Uncle G. Everything will be all right! You know so many beautiful stories. And if you want, you can practice on us!"

Cheesy cream puffs, I actually felt a little BETTER!

I sat down near the two young mice and began to tell them the epic adventures of Homer's *Iliad*.

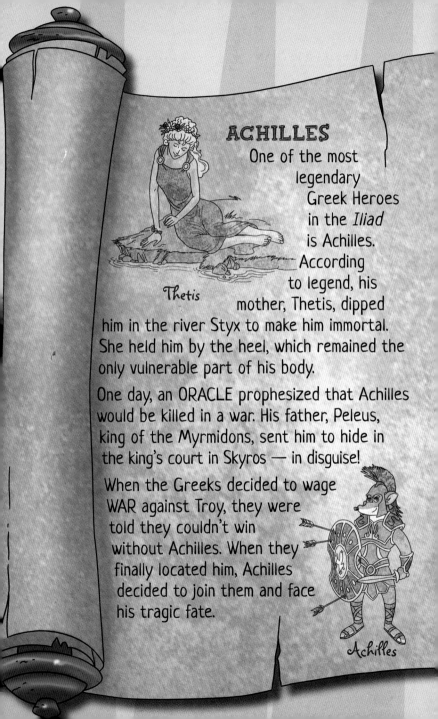

ACHILLES

One of the most legendary Greek Heroes in the *Iliad* is Achilles. According to legend, his mother, Thetis, dipped him in the river Styx to make him immortal. She held him by the heel, which remained the only vulnerable part of his body.

Thetis

One day, an ORACLE prophesized that Achilles would be killed in a war. His father, Peleus, king of the Myrmidons, sent him to hide in the king's court in Skyros — in disguise!

When the Greeks decided to wage WAR against Troy, they were told they couldn't win without Achilles. When they finally located him, Achilles decided to join them and face his tragic fate.

Achilles

THE ILIAD

The events covered in the *Iliad* begin after NINE LONG YEARS OF WAR, during which the Greek army camped outside the walls of Troy without any results.

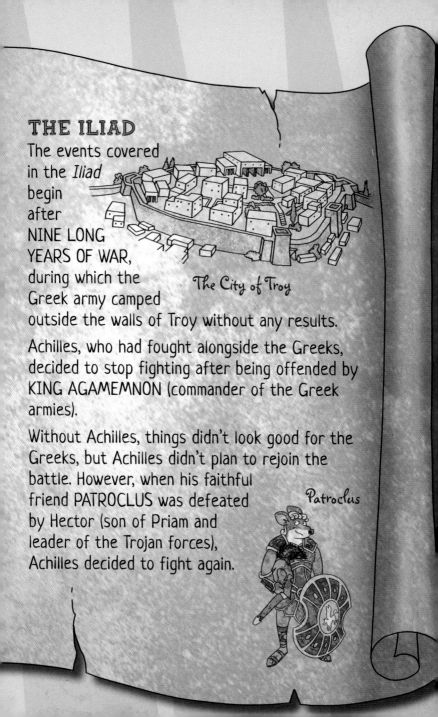

The City of Troy

Achilles, who had fought alongside the Greeks, decided to stop fighting after being offended by KING AGAMEMNON (commander of the Greek armies).

Without Achilles, things didn't look good for the Greeks, but Achilles didn't plan to rejoin the battle. However, when his faithful friend PATROCLUS was defeated by Hector (son of Priam and leader of the Trojan forces), Achilles decided to fight again.

Patroclus

ACHILLES'S RAGE

Achilles's rage

The death of Patroclus filled Achilles with rage! With new armor, Achilles went in search of Hector. In the end, Achilles defeated the Trojan prince in battle, but his rage continued.

Though Achilles's fate is not covered in the *Iliad*, it is said that the vengeful god APOLLO directed the arrow of Paris (Hector's brother) right into ACHILLES'S HEEL, the hero's only weak point. That shot to the heel is how he was ultimately defeated.

THE TROJAN HORSE

According to the tales of Homer, the Greeks devised a sneaky plan to defeat the city of Troy.

The Greeks pretended to retreat, leaving a large WOODEN HORSE outside the city walls as a gift to the gods. The Trojans, believing they had won, brought the horse into the city. What they didn't realize was that there were Greek soldiers hiding inside! That night, the Greeks climbed out of the horse and devastated Troy. That was the end of the city!

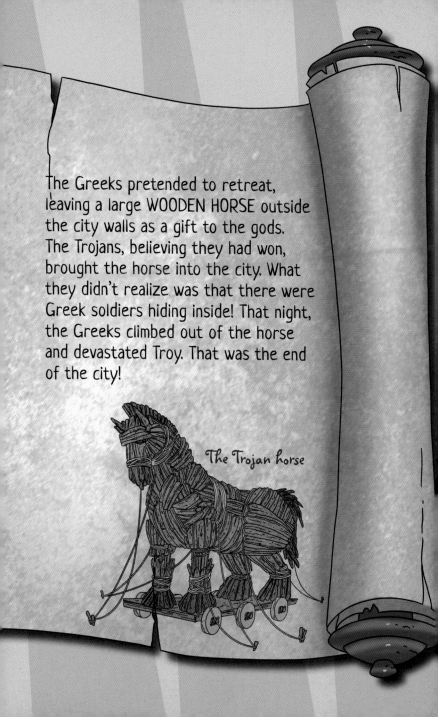

The Trojan horse

BAD IMPRESSION #1!

I practiced my storytelling until SUNSET. After a while, I calmed down. I **actually** thought that everything might go all right that evening . . .

BUT I WaS WrONG — FaBUMOUSELY WrONG!

For starters, Charlemagne and Christopher Columbus both continued to **WaTCH** me threateningly. They wanted to get back to their own times!

Attila was furious and threatened to demousify me every five minutes. Squeak!

And Trap? Well, my cousin just made fun of me. "Work harder, you CHEESEBRAIN, or you'll end up skewered like a mouse kebab!"

This was all really starting to toast my cheese!

I felt like an overinflated **BaLLOON** that was ready to burst, and Trap was really about

Oops!

to make me explode.

Right then, the door to our room slammed open.

BANG!

In a panic, I jumped several feet and hit my head against a shelf!

Youch!

A guard entered and boomed, "Follow me — Helen is waiting!"

We followed him **THROUGH** rooms, hallways, and courtyards full of columns until we reached the banquet hall.

Priam was sitting in the seat of honor. At his side were his wife, Hecuba, and their **sons** and **daughters**. Crusty cheese niblets, there were so many of them!

Among them were the famouse Hector and the **handsome** Paris. I immediately recognized him

because he was gazing lovingly at Helen. That mouse was snout over paws in love!

The guards directed us to sit at a long table. Holey cheese, what a feast! As I stuffed my snout, the mice near me gossiped so much my ears rang from all the chatter.

One of them leaned over to me and whispered, "Hey, did you hear the latest?"

"Huh?"

She rolled her eyes. "EVERYONE in Troy KNOWS!"

"Actually, I just got here . . ." I said.

"Well, everyone is squeaking about how Paris kidnapped Helen. And now she's become his GIRLFRIEND!"

I pretended to be surprised, even though I knew the whole story. "Putrid cheese puffs!" I cried.

"They say that she's already married!" the mouse went on.

"Really? To who?"

"To Menelaus, the king of Sparta!" she squeaked. "It sounds like he's fabumousely JEALOUS . . ."

Did you hear? Blah, blah, blah . . .

Yes, everyone knows! Blah, blah, blah . .

To you, Father!

"Sure as squeaking!" said another rodent.

"**I bet** he'll be here soon with his fleet," one said. "Actually, it's kind of strange that they haven't arrived yet . . ."

They went on filling my ears with Chatter, commenting on Helen's clothing, her jewels, her hair. Then they went on to talk about all the other rodents in the room. WHAT CHATTERBOXES!

Squeeeak, I couldn't take it anymore! I even covered my ears with my paws, but it wasn't enough.

THEY WERE FILLING MY EARS WITH CHATTER!

Blah, blah . . . Ack! Blah, blah . . . Everyone knows!

Blah . . . blah . . . blah . . . blah . . . blah . . . Help! Blah . . . blah . . . blah . . .

I EVEN COVERED MY EARS WITH MY PAWS, BUT IT WASN'T ENOUGH!

Finally, I pretended to have a headache and wrapped a SCARF around my ears!

Moldy mozzarella, finally a bit of silence!

Just then, Helen called me. Then she called me again . . . and then again . . .

But I didn't hear her, because my ears were covered! Rats!

Finally, Trap pinched my tail. "Wake up, she's talking to you!"

Squeak, I had already made bad impression #1!

THEN I WRAPPED A SCARF AROUND MY EARS!

Huh?

How peaceful!

Eh?

Geronacheeeee!

I DIDN'T HEAR PRINCESS HELEN

BAD IMPRESSIONS #2 AND #3!

I jumped to my paws, **unwrapped** the scarf from my head, and quickly headed to the throne. "Um, Your Majesty, forgive me! I was scarfed in the noggin . . . I mean, I was noggined by the scarf . . . I mean, I WRAPPED my head in a scarf!"

In my panic, I tripped on the scarf and it got wrapped around my PaWS. I fell snoutfirst on

the ground, biting my tongue!

Chomp!

And that's how I made bad impression #2!

I got up, redder than the sauce on a double-cheese pizza, and bowed awkwardly before the throne. "**Majemeee!**"

I meant to say "Majesty," but I had bitten my tongue and couldn't talk!

And that's how I made bad impression #3!

I must have set a record: three bad impressions in less than thirty seconds!

Helen raised an **eyebrow**, Paris raised an **eyebrow**, and even Priam raised an **eyebrow**.

They all just stared at me, confused.

Then Paris said, "So you are the new STORYTELLER? Well then, tell us a story!"

I stammered, "Gnagny, gneye gnant gnalk!" (I meant to say, "*Sorry, I can't talk!*")

Priam thundered, "You can't talk? So then sing!"

The kithara player began to tune his instrument:

This doesn't look good . . .

It's very bad!

No, it's a disaster!

Gnagny, gneye gnant gnalk!

PlinG! PlanG! PlonG! PlunG! PlanG!

I broke out in a cold sweat. How could I sing if I couldn't even talk?

Rancid ricotta, how **stressful**!

The kithara player gave me a note, looking at me expectantly. PlinG!

I was quiet for a moment. It seemed to go on FOREVER as my whiskers trembled, my knees knocked, and my swollen tongue stuck to the roof of my mouth.

Then, as usual, Thea came to my rescue.

I have to get him out of this mess!

She stepped forward and bowed GRACIOUSLY before the throne. Then she looked at Priam, Paris, and Hector, batting her eyes. "Noble sirs, please excuse my sister. Your magnificence has intimidated her. She is a simple mouse, and she isn't used to such

Splendor! Please allow me to speak with her to give her some courage."

They agreed.

Thea came up and whispered in my ear. "Geronimo, I will sing instead of you. Just move your mouth and try to keep up! If they find out what we're doing, they'll skewer us like mouse kebabs."

Then she covered her face with a paw and began to sing. Breathless, I moved my mouth, trying to look **inspired** as the kithara player strummed with all his might.

Goddess, sing . . .

"Goddess, sing the rage of Peleus's son Achilles . . ."*

* This is the beginning of the epic poem the *Iliad* by Homer.

But as soon as I said "Achilles," Hector jumped up like he had a **SPRING** under his tail.

"Achilles? Did I hear her say Achilles? I can't stand that braggart! He thinks he's so **SPeciaL**! How dare you squeak his name here!"

I **froze** in fear — and stopped moving my mouth!

Astyanassa noticed right away and squeaked, "Geronache can't sing! She's a **fake**!"

I looked at Thea and she looked at me. Then we both shouted, "*RUUUUUN!*"

Run!

Let's gooooo!

We ran out of the banquet hall as fast as our paws would take us. The guards darted after us, thundering, "Finally, we can skewer someone! These banquets are usually so boring!"

For the love of cheese, I was pretty sure that couldn't have gone worse! But then, during our **ESCAPE**, my wig fell off.

"**Spies!**" the guards hollered, pointing at me. Squeak!

We ran like rats being chased by starved cats, until we finally reached the Cheese-O-Sphere.

I sealed the door, but before beginning the departure procedure, I peeked out the porthole.

The sea outside Troy was full of ships!

Holey cheese, the Greeks had arrived!

The great Trojan War had begun!

We were going to escape just in time!

DESTINATION:

THE TIME OF THE HUNS

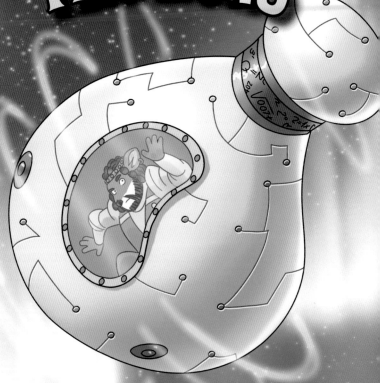

READY, SET, GO!

My whiskers were still trembling when Benjamin shouted, "*HURRY*, Uncle G! We need to begin the departure procedure!"

Bugsy read the information about Attila's time period from the SUPER MANUAL . . . but those pages had been nibbled on, too. Rats!

We all swallowed a spoonful of the *brain essence*, turned upside down, said the amperat equation, and . . . *ZAP*!

There was a flash of light and the time machine began to **spin**. As we were being shaken like smoothies all over again, I thought through everything Bugsy had read us about the **Huns**. They seemed fabumously fierce!

The Huns

The Huns are an ancient NOMADIC Asian population that is believed to have first appeared in the Roman Empire around AD 370, on the shores of the Danube.

HUN

WHAT DID THEY LOOK LIKE?

Historians describe the Huns as frightening, STOCKY warriors with clean-shaven, often scarred cheeks, and legs that bowed outward because they were so often on horseback.

WHAT DID THEY EAT?

According to Roman historian Ammianus Marcellinus, the Huns typically ate the roots of wild herbs as well as SEMI-RAW MEAT that they warmed under their legs as they sat on their horses.

WHERE DID THEY LIVE?

The Huns were nomads without any ties to the land. They spent most of their time on HORSEBACK while fighting — it is said that they also sometimes slept on horseback! When they did stop, they lived in TENTS similar to yurts or in wooden structures, according to some accounts.

Fashion at the Time of the Huns

The Huns wore LEATHER CLOTHES made from wild animal skins, and they carried quivers of ARROWS on their backs. On their feet, they often wore SHEEPSKIN BOOTS. These boots got little use on the ground, though, because the men spent so much time on horseback!

WOMEN'S FASHION

THE LEADER'S WIFE

A WEAVER

A GIRL

It is also said that the Huns RARELY WASHED THEIR CLOTHES — they would just wear them until they wore out!

MEN'S FASHION

THE LEADER OF THE HUNS

A WARRIOR

A BOY

Invincible Warriors

The Huns were GREAT WARRIORS, skilled horsemen, and infallible archers. Even as children, they learned to use their bows and ride horses.

In war, they mostly used BOWS AND ARROWS and SPEARS, with sharp points made of animal bones. In close combat they used iron swords.

The Huns didn't recognize any authority or law. Instead, they followed the leader who guided them in combat. AND THE HUNS KNEW HOW TO BATTLE! Their terrible BATTLE CRIES sparked terror among the enemy ranks.

And, of course, they were truly a fury on horseback!

A HUN WARRIOR ON HORSEBACK

A Bit of History

The Huns were EXTREMELY FEROCIOUS WARRIORS. After conquering the Alani and the Ostrogoths, they forced the Visigoths to flee westward. In the fourth century AD, they established themselves in the areas near the Danube, where they carried out multiple raids in both parts of the Roman Empire.

ATTILA

ATTILA was the Huns' most ferocious leader, but in AD 451 he was defeated by imperial troops during an invasion of Gaul. He then invaded Italy, but was forced to turn back because of famine and sickness within his troops.

After Attila died in AD 453, the Hun Empire rapidly fell.

TICK! TICK! TICK! TICK! TICK! TICK!

When the Cheese-O-Sphere stopped spinning, I felt like a mouse milkshake!

Cheese niblets, my head was still spinning!

As soon as I could see again, I noticed that I was dressed like a Hun warrior. I called over to Attila. "Great Attila, now I will give you the **MEMORY-ERASING ESSENCE** so that you will forget about this adventure outside your time. But before I do, promise me one thing?"

"What is it, rat?" Attila said. "What do you want? You did bring me home, and **Attila** never forgets his debts!"

I got to my knees and begged, "Great and powerful Attila, can you promise that you will not destroy us, demousify us, or **CRUSH US**?"

I put a scroll note in his paw. I'll admit, I'd made it as big as I could, because I wanted to be sure that he wouldn't forget his promise!

"Here is a small **REMINDER** . . ." I squeaked.

Attila gave me his Hun's word of honor that he wouldn't crush us. I finally gave him a spoonful of the memory-erasing essence before he climbed out of the **Cheese-O-Sphere**.

I gave an enormouse sigh of relief. Our mission to bring Attila home had been completed *without any trouble*!

Kindly remember to not destroy, demousify, or crush these mice who have helped me and who have an important mission to carry out.

Signed, Attila the Hun

What do you want, rat?

Remember not to demousify us!

I was about to begin the departure procedure again so we could go on to Charlemagne's time, when I heard a strange sound . . .

TICK!

TICK! TICK!

TICK! TICK! TICK!

What could it be?

Maybe **RAIN**?

Maybe hail?

Then the Cheese-O-Sphere began to roll every which way, like a ball!

Cheese and crackers, what was happening?

Because of all that **rolling**, the door of the Cheese-O-Sphere opened and we tumbled out like a can of spilled cheese balls! I blinked and looked around. Moldy mozzarella — we were right in the middle of a battle!

The Roman army was lined up on one side, and a horde of Huns on horseback was arriving on the

THE CHEESE-O-SPHERE
ROLLED TO THE RIGHT . . .

IT ROLLED TO THE LEFT . . .

IT ROLLED DOWNWARD . . .

IT ROLLED UPWARD

SQUEEEAK!

SO MUCH ROLLING!

other side, launching a barrage of arrows!

Rats, that's what all those *tick* sounds were — arrows!

I squeaked, "For all the Hun Havarti, what in the world went wrong this time?" I couldn't take it anymore!

Bugsy tugged on my paw. "Uncle G,

Tops ate half of the pages about the Huns! I could only read about how they were **terrible**, **tremendous**, terrifying warriors, who were super-skilled at horseback riding and piercing their enemies with arrows!"

We all yelled at once, "Squeeeeeeak! We're in trouble!"

Meanwhile, the Hun warriors on horseback were coming closer and closer. What a feline fright! We tried to get back inside the Cheese-O-Sphere, but the horses kept bumping it, making it roll around like a billiard **ball**.

I yelled, "Hey, wait for us!"

HEY, YOU ROTTEN ROQUEFORT!

Trap shouted after the Cheese-O-Sphere, "Hey, you ugly, rotten Roquefort, if I catch you, I'll teach you a lesson!"

Just then, a **Hun** who was as big as a bus passed really close to us. Rats, he thought that **I** had said that to **him**!

He planted himself in front of me and **THUNDERED**, "How dare you call me an '**ugly, rotten Roquefort**'? I am Giganteron, the great Attila's general! Warriors, grab this rodent — no, grab them all! I can make a nice LINING for my boots out of their fur!"

Hey! How dare they?

WHITER THAN A BALL OF MOZZARELLA

The Huns were on us in a flash. They were coming from every direction, and they were very **ferocious**!

Thea looked at me and exclaimed, "Geronimo, you're whiter than a **ball of mozzarella**! Are you going to faint?"

I wobbled on my paws. "Maybe I'm going to faint . . . yes, I'm about to faint . . . **I'm faaaintiiing!**"

The last thing I saw was my friends being captured and tied up like smoked cheese. Then everything went dark.

When I opened my **EYES** again, I was also tied up, facing backward on a saddle.

I had a headache, and my snout was sore. I

must have hit my head when I fainted. In front of me was that **Hun warrior**, Giganteron, who threatened, "Now I will take you to *him*. He will take care of you! He will destroy you, he will demousify you, he will **CRUSH** you! He will teach you not to provoke a Hun. Did you know that he is so terrifying that where he walks, the grass no longer grows?"

I suddenly understood — "he" was Attila!

I almost felt a bit relieved!

Maybe Attila still had that reminder I had given him?

Maybe he would remember his **promise** not to demousify us, crush us, or destroy us?

The Huns unloaded us in front of a wooden building on a platform supported by pillars. All around was a large, fenced-in area, where not a single blade of grass was growing.

"You see?" Giganteron thundered. "I told you

that where he walks, *grass* no longer grows!"

Squeak — that was Attila's house! I recognized it from the Super Manual. I was about to find out if he remembered his promise.

What fright, what anxiety, what stress!

Giganteron and his companions pushed us inside Attila's house, **POKING** our tails with their sharp swords.

"Ouch!" Bugsy and Benjamin cried out in unison.

"Cheddarbreath!" yelled Trap.

"Don't you know who I am?!" hollered Charlemagne.

"Paws down, **FOOL**!" squeaked Thea.

Me? I was squeakless. My tongue had stuck to the top of my mouth in **FEAR**!

Suddenly, there he was: Attila. He was seated on his throne, staring at us menacingly.

My whiskers wobbled uncontrollably at the

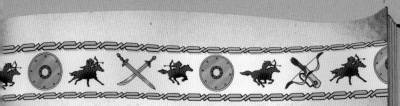

The Huns' Houses

The Huns' houses were made of WOOD planks that were DECORATED according to the owners' tastes and positioned in a particular symmetrical order.

ATTILA'S PALACE was also made of wood. It was quite large and took up a lot of space. The external enclosure was made of a wooden plank FENCE that contained other wood houses. The only stone structures were the bathrooms.

Separate houses were assigned to each of Attila's wives. The house of the preferred queen was made of thick wood with round columns etched with beautiful decorations.

sight of him! He seemed even scarier than when he first stepped off the Cheese-O-Sphere.

He didn't recognize us because of the MEMORY-ERASING ESSENCE, but some trace of our faces must have stayed in his brain. "Rats, tell me, where have I seen your silly snouts before? Maybe on the battlefield? Have I CAPTURED you already? No, that's impossible — you're still alive! Maybe you have been here as ambassadors? Or are you SPIES? Come now, rats, squeak!"

I wanted to tell Attila about the reminder that he had stuck in his belt, but I didn't have a chance.

Giganteron punched his chest with a paw and bowed his snout in respect. Then he thundered, "Oh, great Attila, I captured them on the battlefield. I think they're spies!"

Attila stepped forward and felt my (bony) arm, then touched my (soft) stomach and muttered, "They don't seem like warriors, and they definitely don't seem like Huns. They are too puny! You're right, Giganteron — they must be **enemy spies**!"

Giganteron exclaimed, "Fabumouse! Can I destroy them, demousify them, **CRUSH** them with my own paws? They called me an 'ugly, rotten Roquefort.' I can't let that slide!"

I tried to apologize. "I, um, I didn't mean — I mean — you're not an ugly, rotten Roquefort . . . I mean, congratulations on those **muscles**! You're as tough as an aged cheese rind!"

I'LL GIVE *YOU* A CHEESE RIND!

Giganteron looked **furious**. "Rat, I'll give *you* a cheese rind! You're no Huns, you're all spies!"

Trap jumped forward. "We're not spies, we're Huns!" He gestured to me. "This one is a bit weak in the muscle department, but I, on the other paw, am all muscle."

Charlemagne looked indignant. "Me, a spy? I'm the empe —"

Thea jumped up and clapped a paw over his mouth. "He is the LEADER of a faraway Hun tribe and has come here to pay homage to the great Attila."

Then she turned to Giganteron and batted her BIG purple EYES.

"You great musclemouse, please don't be offended. In our tribe, the phrases 'rotten Roquefort' and 'aged cheese rind' are compliments! They mean '*You're so strong*' and 'You're so courageous and fascinating'! You really do seem strong and courageous, I must say. Plus, you have fabumouse whiskers!"

I noticed that Giganteron had turned **red**. "Oh! They're compliments? Well then, I guess I won't destroy you . . . this time."

But Attila didn't seem convinced. He narrowed

You great musclemouse . . .
what nice whiskers!

Umm . . .

his eyes and asked, "So, who are you? What do you want? Where have you come from?"

Thea responded before I could even squeak. "We are from the Mousoski Cheesoski Hun tribe, and we come from distant Mouseland. Word of the great Attila and his **FIERCE WARRIORS** has reached us there."

How smart! How brave! Thea always knows exactly how to get me out of trouble.

Attila snickered. "You're **Huns**? Very well then — **prove it**!" He turned to the other Huns. "Give them some horses and bows and arrows!"

I remembered what Bugsy had read about the Huns being skilled horse riders who learned to ride and shoot arrows as young **mice**.

Next, I remembered that I don't know how to ride a horse! I am the world champion of extraordinary falls, and I hold the **record** in horse-related mistakes and falling in fresh manure!

Rancid ricotta, I was in even more trouble than I'd thought!

Luckily, Thea offered to show her **skills** first. She is a champion horseback rider. She recently won the **Mouse Equestrian Grand Prize**! Unsurprisingly, she's also very good with a bow.

Sure as squeaking, she was **MARVEMOUSE**! The warriors applauded, and the women of the village looked at her admiringly.

"Holey cheese, where did you learn to ride so well?" Attila asked.

Marvemouse!

What technique!

What style!

Bugsy and Benjamin were **fabumouse**, too. They had both been horseback riding all their lives, and Thea had taught them to use a bow and arrow!

CHARLEMAGNE was the best of all. He galloped proudly across the field, made his horse rear up on its hind legs, and shot three arrows directly into the bull's-eye!

Even Christopher Columbus did a good job! He didn't hit the **CENTER** of the bull's-eye, but he did well for an older gentlemouse.

When it was his turn, Trap stood up on the horse and did some incredible acrobatics. Oh, for the love of cheese!

With every twirl he shouted, "Hop! Hop! Hop!" He even rode upside down, balancing on just one paw. I had to admit, it was truly fabumouse!

Everyone applauded wildly. "MOUSETASTIC!"

Trap has had a thousand different jobs in

Hop!

his life: cook, magician, joke store owner, **USELESS** invention salesmouse — he even worked as a juggler in the circus!

I, on the other paw, have only ever had one job: writer and editor of **The Rodent's Gazette**.

The sports I am best at are **1** lifting a pen, and **2** writing the fastest! Well, I'm also pretty good at **3** munching on chocolates filled with cream and Gorgonzola! Oh, I forgot! When I was a little mouselet in elementary school, I **WON** a marbles tournament . . .

LIFTING A PEN

WRITING THE FASTEST

MUNCHING ON
CHOCOLATES

Other than that, I am the least SPORTY mouse around!

When it was finally my turn to demonstrate my skills, I tried to sneak away, but Giganteron grabbed me and planted me on the horse's saddle.

I tried to explain that I'm an intellectual mouse, but he shoved a bow and three arrows in my paw as the horse galloped off — with me on its back!

"*Geronimo*, try to stay in the saddle!" Thea yelled.

Benjamin tried to encourage me. "Come on, Uncle G! You can do it!"

I tried my very best, but when I attempted to shoot the arrows, one missed the target and hit Giganteron's tail. The other two somehow landed in my tail! Youch!

To distract the public, I tried a fancy, Trap-like maneuver but ended up hanging by the horse's tail. He didn't like that, so he **STOPPED** short and accidentally launched me into the air. I flew spectacularly and landed right in the center of the bull's-eye — headfirst!

Holey cheese balls, what a blow!

Let's see what you can do!

Argh!

GERONIMO ON HORSEBACK:

WHEN I TRIED TO SHOOT THE ARROW, ONE MISSED THE TARGET AND LANDED RIGHT IN GIGANTERON'S TAIL.

THE OTHER TWO ARROWS LANDED IN MY TAIL! WHO KNOWS HOW!

I TRIED ONE OF TRAP'S FANCY MANEUVERS, BUT WAS LEFT HANGING BY THE HORSE'S TAIL!

A REAL CHEESEBRAIN!

THE HORSE STOPPED SHORT AND ACCIDENTALLY LAUNCHED ME FORWARD.

I FLEW SPECTACULARLY THROUGH THE AIR AT TOP SPEED . . .

. . . AND LANDED WITH MY HEAD RIGHT IN THE CENTER OF THE BULL'S-EYE! SQUEAK, WHAT A BLOW!

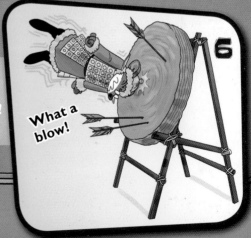

They Are Huns . . . You Are a Nuisance!

The point of my Hun helmet had gotten stuck so deeply in the target that it took **two** enormouse Huns to pull me out!

The whole tribe burst out laughing. What a cheesebrain I am sometimes!

Just then, Attila **STARED** at me seriously

Come on, pull!

Hee, hee, hee!

Ha, ha, ha!

Ho, ho, ho!

and then declared, "Rat, they know what they are doing with horses and a bow! So they are **HUNS**! You, on the other paw, are a nuisance, so you must be a spy. I will **DESTROY** you!"

Giganteron rubbed his paws together. "Ooh, can I keep his fur? I can line my boots and my hat!"

I threw myself at Attila's paws, *crying*, "Have pity! I'm too fond of my fur!

"I am a nuisance, but I'm not a spy!" I went on. "Rodent's honor! I am an intellectual, a writer! I am not a **WARRIOR** — that's why I can't ride horses!"

Have pityyyy!

Attila waved a paw. "It doesn't matter. I've already decided that I will destroy you, and so **I will destroy you**! Attila always keeps his word!"

Suddenly, I got an idea. "Before I'm destroyed, can I ask for one final **WiSH**?"

The crowd of Huns began to chant, "**WiSH! WiSH! WiSH!**"

Attila stared at me. "All right . . . but it doesn't count if your wish is not to be destroyed, demousified, or CRUSHED!"

"What about the one where I get to live until I'm one hundred seventy-three, does that count?" I asked.

Attila narrowed his eyes. He wasn't amused. "That one doesn't count, either."

With my whiskers trembling and my teeth chattering, I said, "Okay, then can I ask you to read the piece of paper tucked in your belt out loud, in front of everyone? Then, if you want, you can destroy me!"

Attila thundered, "Attila always keeps his word! I'll read it, and then **I'll destroy you**!"

Attila took the little reminder that I had given him from his belt and read it out loud.

As soon as Attila FINISHED reading, **Giganteron** rubbed his paws together, "Okay, now let me destroy him!"

But Attila looked at him with menacing **EYES**. "Didn't you hear what I said just a moment ago?

ATTILA ALWAYS KEEPS HIS WORD!"

Attila paused, looking at the paper again. "On this scroll, it is written that I promised **NOT** to destroy him. Even if I don't remember, a promise is a promise! No one will destroy this mouse or his friends, or they will have to face me! *Are we clear?*"

At that point I stammered, "N-n-no one will destroy me, you said? Crusty cheese rinds, what a relief!"

THEN I FAINTED THEN I FAINTED FAINTED THEN I FAINTED FAINTED FAINTED THEN I FAINTED FAINTED FAINTED FAINTED FAINTED

Aaaack!

I woke up many hours later, when I heard a voice calling me. "**RAAAAT!**"

I opened my eyes and saw Giganteron's menacing snout! Squeak!

I nearly jumped out of my fur and yelled, "Rats, don't destroy me! Don't turn me into **lining** for your boots! I'm too fond of my fur!"

Giganteron burst out laughing. "Rat, you really are such a scaredy-mouse! I'm not here to destroy you. I'm here to wake you up. Attila is waiting!"

A MOST MYSTERIOUS MYSTERY!

When I entered Attila's house, all my **friends** were there, waiting for me. They were seated on soft embroidered pillows.

Holey cheese, I was so relieved to see them!

Attila greeted me cordially. Well, almost.

He gave me a slap on the shoulder that would have **knocked** over an ox. "Rats, I don't remember why I promised not to destroy you, but I promised, and I will keep my word. But —"

"But?" I asked.

"But," he repeated.

"But what?!" **WE ALL YELLED**.

"But you must help me solve a most mysterious mystery!"

Trap grinned. "No worries, ol' Attila! This

cheesebrain over here is great at solving mysteries!"

How did I get into these messes?

What if I couldn't solve the mystery this time? What would happen? *SQUEEAK!*

"Attila," I asked quietly, "if I manage to solve your mystery, will you let us **LEAVE**?"

He scratched his snout and twisted his whiskers thoughtfully.

Beats me!

Huh?

You need to solve a mystery!

Who knows?

Then he nodded firmly. "It's a deal! You have my word. If you solve the mystery I will let you leave. But if you're not able to solve it, **I will destroy you**!"

Rat-munching rattlesnakes!

"What kind of mystery is it?" I asked, trying to sound brave.

Attila lowered his voice. "Shhhh! No one can know what happened. Something I care about deeply has disappeared!"

Bugsy squeaked up, "What is it? **Jewels?** Gold? A precious crown?"

"No, no, none of that!" Attila said. "It's a very precious object: a **SWORD**!"

Trap shrugged. "But, Attila, ol' buddy, ol' pal, why don't you just have another one made? There must be a **blacksmith** who can do that!"

"Impossible!" Attila cried. "That sword is **unique**! It's very old and extremely precious!

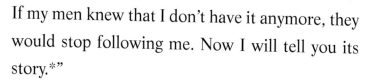

If my men knew that I don't have it anymore, they would stop following me. Now I will tell you its story.*"

While Attila told the story, I thought, and thought, and thought. Cheese niblets, who could it have been? Who would want to steal a sword? Maybe a political enemy?

I asked, "Attila, do you have **enemies**?"

He burst out laughing. "What a funny mouse! I have many enemies: the Romans, the leaders of other tribes, enemies of all shapes and sizes, even though I've destroyed so many of them!"

"*Hmmmm,*" I mused. "Where did you keep the sword?"

"In this chest," Attila answered, gesturing with his paw.

I noticed that the lock had not been forced open.

"Who was allowed to touch the chest?" I asked.

---

* The Byzantine historian, Priscus of Panium, tells the story of the legend of Attila's sword.

THE LEGEND OF
ATTILA'S SWORD

One day, a poor shepherd noticed that one of his cows was injured. He anxiously followed the traces of blood the animal had left, and they led him to a sword that was almost completely buried in the earth.

The shepherd, who was afraid of keeping or selling such a magnificent object, brought the sword to Attila. Attila immediately recognized it as a sacred object belonging to the Roman god of war, Mars. The sword had disappeared many years before, and it was believed to be lost forever!

Attila had no doubt of the importance of that discovery. As a result, he convinced himself that he was now the leader of the entire world, and that the sword would guarantee his victory in all battles.

"**NO ONE!**" Attila cried. "I mean, aside from me, my wives, my children, and my faithful Giganteron, no one is allowed in here or —"

Hmmm, the lock wasn't forced!

"Or you'd destroy them!" Bugsy and Benjamin interrupted. "We know, you destroy everything and everyone, holey cheese!"

Attila looked at them with wide **EYES**. Moldy mozzarella, I thought he was furious — but instead, he burst out laughing.

"You cute little mice! You are fearless, like my youngest son. He always says what he thinks, too! He is the only one who doesn't fear me. You three could be friends!"

I wanted to get back on topic. "So you said

wives?" I asked. "How many of them are there?"

Attila seemed to be thinking for a moment. Then he threw his paws in the air. "Well, there are quite a few. Anyway, I'm about to marry another one. She's known as **Ildico**." He puffed out his chest with pride. "Did you know that I even received a proposal from Honoria, the sister of Roman emperor Valentinian the third? I suppose I have a certain mousely appeal!"

I am his favorite!

I'm the nicest!

I'm the prettiest!

I'm the strongest!

I'm the most chic!

I'm the most refined!

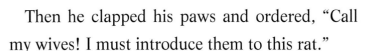

Then he clapped his paws and ordered, "Call my wives! I must introduce them to this rat."

The rodents entered, all of them dressed in super-elegant clothing and holding their snouts in the air.

Attila said, "So this is **Ildico** — I'm going to marry her next!"

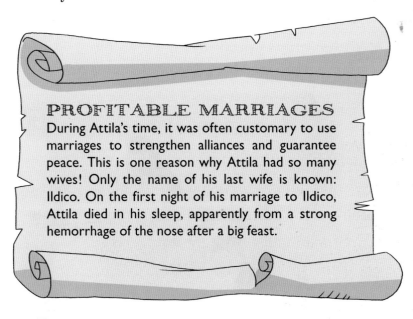

PROFITABLE MARRIAGES
During Attila's time, it was often customary to use marriages to strengthen alliances and guarantee peace. This is one reason why Attila had so many wives! Only the name of his last wife is known: Ildico. On the first night of his marriage to Ildico, Attila died in his sleep, apparently from a strong hemorrhage of the nose after a big feast.

GO, CONQUER, AND COME BACK A WINNER!

Attila's wives began to **complain**. "Attila, my dear, when are you leaving for another conquest?"

One of them squeaked, "Husband of mine — I mean, husband of ours — the SWORD will protect you. You can't lose! So go, conquer, and come back! But most of all, come back a winner like you always do."

Attila turned to his wives, smiling. "Please excuse us! Your dear Attila needs to talk about important matters with this rat."

As soon as they had left, Attila whispered, "Did you hear that, rat? Even they believe that that sword makes me INVINCIBLE! I need to find it!"

I nodded. "I promise, I will do my best to help find it."

When I said good-bye to Attila, he placed a **MEDAL** around my neck. "Rat, use this. When rodents see it, every house and every tent will be open to you!"

Then we all LEFT. As soon as we were alone, I said, "We need to split up. I'll carry out the official investigation. The rest of you should **MINGLE** with the local mice. Don't get noticed, and keep your eyes and ears open. We'll meet back in our tent at **nightfall!**"

I began to walk through the field, where everyone was busy with their wagons and tents, preparing for the night. Some were cooking, some were caring for horses, some were fixing fences. For a moment, I forgot that I was in the encampment of the most **FEARED** warriors of all time!

Without realizing it, I had wandered away from the encampment. I found myself on a little hill where I could observe the landscape. And I began to think . . . and think . . . and think . . . and think . . . and think . . . and think . . . and think . . . and think . . . and think . . . and think . . . and think . . . and think . . . and think . . . until I got an idea!

I headed to Attila's house. It was the only grassless place around. There, the soft, mushy ground would give me exactly what I was looking for — TRACES of the sword thief!

But when I reached Attila's house, I was distracted by a rodent, whining desperately with tears pouring down his snout.

"Oh, poor meeeee! What a disaster! What a thankless job! **Enough!** I can't take it anymore — I'm going to quit!"

"Can I help you?" I asked.

Between one **SOB** and the next, the mouse dried his tears on my sleeve and blew his nose on my coat. Holey cheese, how gross! Then he

Waaaaah!

explained, "Alas, no one can help me. I am Attila's gardener!"

"But why are you so upset? That sounds like a nice job," I said.

He sobbed, BLOWING his nose on my fur. "You know what they say about Attila? Where he walks, grass no longer grows? Well, it's true! Every time he walks through, I need to replant all the grass! I can't do it anymore! It's a terrible job!"

I patted him on the shoulder. "Friend, I have an idea. Go home and rest. This time, I will plant the grass. Sound good?"

When the grateful gardener left, I sprinkled some grass seed on the ground and went in search of traces of the sword thief. I didn't want anyone to get suspicious, so I tried to look like a gardener.

There were many pawprints in front of the house, including ours. My fellow travelers and I had also passed that way to talk to Attila not so long ago.

In back of the house, there were just two lines of prints. These were different than all the others — they were very small. **HOW STRANGE!**

I took a closer look. The pawprints leading

Hmm, very strange!

toward the house were not very deep. But the prints that were going away from the house sunk deeper into the **EARTH**.

HOW STRANGE!

Maybe whoever left the house was carrying something heavy? Maybe it was . . . the **SWORD**?

But how did the thief manage to enter and exit? There were no doors or windows on the back!

I began to tap at the walls, looking for a secret passage. **Tap tap! Tap tap!** But I didn't find anything. Rats!

Then I slipped under the house, which sat on top of an elevated platform. I continued to tap: **Tap tap! Tap tap!**

Eventually, one of the boards went TOCK! I pushed it and it moved, letting a bit of light through. I had found a passageway!

Here's a passageway!

Hmmm . . .

Now I just had to find the **guilty** rodent! I followed the tracks for a while, but then I lost them when they mixed in with all the other villagers' prints. Holey cheese balls, what a **disaster**! Was all my tracking for nothing?

In low spirits, I went back to our tent, where my **friends** were waiting.

Sigh!

When Bugsy saw me she squeaked, "So, Uncle G, did you **find** anything?"

"Not much, unfortunately," I said. "Here's what I **DISCOVERED**:

1) The sword thief did not enter through the front door of Attila's house! (So that means he was sneaking around.)

2) The thief used a passageway under the floor that leads right to the spot where the sword was kept! (So he knew the house, the location of the sword, and the right time to act without being discovered.)

3) The passageway is very narrow! (So the thief is really skinny!)

4) He left tiny prints in the mud that were not very deep! (So the thief is light and has small paws!)"

Thea sighed. "I didn't find out much by talking to Attila's wives, either. But here's what I did **DISCOVER**:

1) During the last few weeks, not one of Attila's wives entered his house. They are all angry with him, because they're jealous of his new girlfriend, Ildico.

2) Ildico never went to Attila unaccompanied by her maids. That is the custom of the people – before marriage, the husband can never be alone with his girlfriend!

So none of Attila's wives committed the robbery!"

Charlemagne and Christopher Columbus had also asked some questions around town. Columbus tried to update me on his discoveries, but Charlemagne interrupted. "Quiet, Christopher. I will speak, since I am the emperor! We mixed in with Attila's warriors and guards. And here's what we **DISCOVERED** . . .

1) There are always two soldiers in front of Attila's door. Since they're fond of their fur, neither one closed an eye during their shift – not even for a second!

2) The only moment the soldiers abandoned their post was during the last battle, when they captured us.

3) Right before the battle, Attila had suddenly disappeared! (He was traveling through time with us!) The guards were looking for him everywhere.

So the sword disappeared right before the battle! No one left the grounds from that moment on. Beforehand, they were surrounded by enemies; after, Attila ordered that no one leave the camp!

That means that the sword is still here somewhere!"

Swiss cheese on rye, this was all very, very interesting! But I still didn't understand one big, important thing: Who had stolen the sword? **WHO? Who? WHOOOO?** Trap rubbed his belly, satisfied. He let out

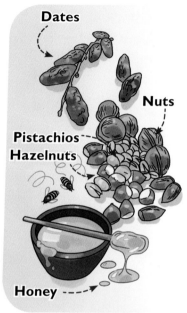

Dates

Nuts

Pistachios
Hazelnuts

Honey

Slurp!

a big burp. "**BURP!** I, umm, inquired among the **COOKS** and checked their provisions. I didn't find anything unusual, but I discovered that these **Huns** aren't half-bad when it comes to food! They have lots of treats from the *East*: candied sweets, dried fruit, and even honey. *Yum!*"

I rolled my eyes. "Trap, you never change. All you can think about is **stuffing your snout!** We need to find the sword and get our tails in gear!"

"Don't worry, Uncle G," Benjamin squeaked up. "Bugsy and I **ASKED** some of the young mice around the encampment . . . and we figured out who stole the **SWORD**!"

Thundering cattails, I couldn't believe my ears!

Benjamin whispered in my ear, "The thief is . . . pssssst . . . pssst . . . pssst pssst . . . pssst . . . pssst . . . pssst . . . pssst . . . pssst . . . psst . . . pssst . . . pssst! But can you promise that he won't get punished?"

Pssst! Pssst!

Hmmm . . .

WHO STOLE MY SWORD?

At that moment, Giganteron arrived. He entered our tent, THUNDERING, "Rats, time is up! If you have found what you needed, good. Otherwise, it's time to face your fate!"

Then he led us to Attila, who looked on edge. "So? Who stole my sword?"

Thea held up a paw. "Don't worry, Attila, we found out who did it! Actually, these two young

Who? Who? Who?

mice figured it out! As soon as you stop yelling, they will tell you."

Attila's snout stretched into a smile. "Well done! If you're right, I will give you anything you ask for. **Attila's word!**"

Bugsy said, with a trembling voice, "The sword was stolen by . . ."

"BY?"

"BY . . ."

Spit it out!

"By who?" Attila cried. "Have courage, spit it out!"

Benjamin said, "If we tell you, can you promise that you won't punish him? We convinced him to confess, but we also promised that he won't be punished. He's our friend!"

Attila turned as red as the sauce on a double-cheese pizza. For a moment, we all thought that he would **explode** and destroy us.

Instead, he burst out laughing. "Ha, ha, ha!

"What clever mouselets! Now I have to **keep my word**. If we recover the sword, whoever stole it will not be punished. Now tell me who it is at once!"

Bugsy **squeaked**, "Okay, friend, you can come out!"

You can come out, friend!

What?

CRRREAK!

At that moment, silence fell over the room.

We all heard a creaking. **Crrreak!**

We looked around. Who could it be? Then the carpet lifted and a floorboard moved!

A little paw poked out of the floor . . .

Then another . . .

Then two honey-colored ears . . .

Then a little mouse with eyes as dark as blackberries, two skinny paws, and a head of *wild hair* popped out.

It was Attila's youngest son! He looked at his father proudly and said, "Father, I took the sword because I am tired of all these **wars**. I've had enough destruction! I'm also tired of having a yard where not even one blade of grass can grow. It's worse than being surrounded by caged cats!"

Enough destruction!

ATTILA'S SON!

Attila looked thoughtful. "I will not punish you, because I gave my word to your friends. And I have to admit, you were courageous and quick, taking my SWORD without being discovered! But the time has come to give it back to me."

The little mouse put his little paws into the hole in the ground and pulled out Attila's sword.

Benjamin and Bugsy ran to hug their friend.

Give me a paw!

Thanks, friend!

"You were fabumously brave," Benjamin squeaked. "And thanks to you, we can finally leave!"

Attila's son smiled. "Well, I was sorry that I took the sword. Stealing is never the right way to solve a problem."

Trap stepped forward. "Okay, enough of all this sweetness, all this chatter, all this time-wasting! We haven't talked about the most important thing — when do we eat? I'm as famished as a feline!"

When do we eat?

Attila burst out laughing. "You heard the mouse: enough chatter, let's party!"

He clapped his paws, and in a flash an enormouse Hun banquet was organized.

WHAT A STOMACHACHE!

The banquet was marvemouse. Everyone but Attila ate off precious, beautifully DECORATED plates of gold and silver. He chose to use simple wood and terra-cotta plates.

The plates were precious, but the food that was served was, well . . . not meant for rodents like us.

To be honest, it was terrible — especially the raw meat WARMED AND

PRESERVED on horseback. Yuck!

We didn't want to offend **Attila**, so we tried to eat everything. But I could tell it was all a bit aged. Well, more than aged. The food had all gone bad! Holey cheese! Before long, we started to feel sick!

Rancid ricotta, what a **stomachache**!

We all scampered out of Attila's house in search of a bathroom!

Or a bedpan!

Or a bush!

Squeeeeak! What a stomachache!

Squeak, what a stomachache!

It was a looooong night.

The next morning, everyone was as pale as mozzarella, with knees as soft and wobbly as rotten Brie!

Benjamin and Bugsy really looked bad. They had DARK CIRCLES under their eyes, their ears drooped, and their whiskers were limp.

Thea and I looked at each other. We both knew what we had to do.

Squeak!

What a stomachache!

Thea clapped her paws. "We're going take you back home, **to the present**. You both need to rest up and get well!"

They squeaked in protest, but Trap knew how to convince them. "Do you want me to call the **shaman**? He lives right here! I am sure he will get you feeling better in no time, maybe with a nice, **awful-tasting** herbal tea."

Bugsy and Benjamin turned even paler. "No, no, not the shaman!" Bugsy cried. "We'd much rather **GO BACK** home to Aunt Sweetfur!"

Trap flicked my ear and grinned. "See how convincing I was?"

I ignored him. The important thing was to get Benjamin and Bugsy immediately to present-day New Mouse City. I was worried about them!

In this time period, mice hadn't developed a lot of cures or treatments. A simple illness like a **Stomachache** could be really dangerous!

I patted Benjamin's ears. "Good. Aunt Sweetfur will keep you warm and make you **CHAMOMILE TEA**. She will tell you fabumouse stories to pass the time. Nobody **cuddles** the way she does! I know you'll be feeling better really soon. Rodent's honor!"

Now the time had come for us to say good-bye to Attila.

"Thank you for your hospitality," I said.

He scrutinized us one by one, looking at our **EYES**. "You really are weak! You can't even handle a little Hun banquet? We Huns have **iron stomachs**! But it seems like you Huns from Mouse Island are really rather fragile rodents . . ."

Attila's youngest son said good-bye sadly, muttering, "I wish I could go with you!"

I smiled. "Who knows, maybe one day we will see each other again. Mouse Island isn't as **FAR AWAY** as it seems!"

You are fragile rodents, you Huns from Mouse Island!

Umm . . .

INVISIBLE . . .
TOO INVISIBLE!

Finally, we **HEADED** back to the Cheese-O-
Sphere. It was still right where we had left it,
perfectly invisible in the middle of the steppe.

It was almost too invisible . . .

I didn't see it — and banged my snout right into
its side! **BANG!**

Bang!

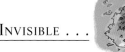

We **climbed** aboard and repeated the **departure procedure**. This time, we didn't even have to read aloud from the Super Manual. Instead, each of us concentrated on Professor von Volt's laboratory. Then we all took a spoonful of the **BRAIN ESSENCE**, turned upside down, and recited the amperat equation. In a flash, we **rematerialized** in the Incredible Airship with a bang.

When we opened the Cheese-O-Sphere door, the professor greeted us with open arms. "You're back already? You were so **QUICK**! I think you've beaten the record for speedy time travel! **Truly mousetastic!**"

As Charlemagne and Christopher Columbus stepped out of the **time machine**, I said, "I'm sorry to

You're back!

disappoint you, Professor. As you can see, the mission isn't done yet. We only returned three out of the five time travelers. These two still have to go back."

That's when the professor noticed how **TERRIBLE** we all looked.

"Moldy mozzarella, how could I not have noticed before? You all look worse than rats trapped in a cat cage! Come, rest. I have a specially equipped area for travelers' speedy recovery!"

I put up a paw. "Thank you, Professor, but we're going to continue our mission at once. We only came to bring Benjamin and Bugsy home. Can you take them back to Aunt Sweetfur?"

We gave both mouselets enormouse hugs. "Stay strong — you'll feel better soon! You have to be in good shape to celebrate when we finish this journey through time."

Before we left, Professor von Volt pulled me aside. "Geronimo, how is the Cheese-O-Sphere working? I didn't have time to test it thoroughly, and —"

"The Cheese-O-Sphere has some small defects," I said, trying not to alarm him. "The departure procedure is a little too *complicated*!"

"Yes. I knew you would have some issues," Professor von Volt said. "While you've been gone, I have been working hard to get some of those worked out. I think you'll be very **pleased** with the changes."

"That sounds **great**!" I squeaked. "And do you happen to have another copy of the SUPER MANUAL? Tops munched on it!"

The professor frowned. "I'm sorry, I don't have any other *copies*. But if you give me five

minutes, I'll see what I can do to fix the problem. Meanwhile, take a little break." He pressed a button, and a series of hidden doors opened. Out came relaxing massage **chairs**, cooling fans, and refreshing drinks. Thundering cattails, it was amazing!

Five minutes later, we all felt **SO MUCH BETTER**.

Professor von Volt was really a fabumouse inventor! He had managed to get us back on our paws in five minutes flat!

The professor came back into the room, looking **SATISFIED**.

We all entered the Cheese-O-Sphere. Professor von Volt opened a **SMALL DOOR** and explained, "You see this? It's the **quantico-cheeso brain** of the Cheese-O-Sphere. Basically, it's the most vital part. I programmed it to bring you directly to **CHARLEMAGNE'S** court, and then to Christopher Columbus's ship. Now everything should go as smoothly as melted mozzarella! To operate the Cheese-O-Sphere now, just say the name of the destination."

"So we won't have to say the amperat equation anymore?" I asked hopefully.

The professor smiled. "No!"

"Or turn upside down?"

This is the quantico-cheeso brain!

"No, not that, either!"

"And we don't have to take the BRAIN ESSENCE anymore?" I went on.

A MYSTERIOUS expression crossed the professor's snout. "Ah, I thought up a way to give you all a single dose and be done with it. Come with me!"

As we left the Cheese-O-Sphere, he said, "Line up along here, please."

Holey cheese, we were very confused — but we obeyed. Professor von Volt knows what he's doing! A moment later, five huge needles full of brain essence popped out of five hidden doors and . . . ZAP! Professor von Volt shot them right in our tails!

We yelled, "Ack! Eeek! Ooh! Ow! Ouch!"

The professor clapped his paws, satisfied. "Now the procedure is much simpler. Aren't you happy?"

I massaged my tail, muttering "Umm, thanks, Professor von Volt. We're very happy."

Von Volt whispered in my ear, "Geronimo, the only thing that you need to remember is the MEMORY-ERASING ESSENCE. You must make sure that Charlemagne and Christopher Columbus forget about their adventures through time!"

I reassured him with a smile. Then we all boarded the Cheese-O-Sphere again and squeaked, "Destination: Aachen! To Charlemagne's court!"

There was the usual boom, the usual FLASH OF LIGHT, and the Cheese-O-Sphere took off, shaking in its usual way!

The last thing I saw from the porthole was Professor von Volt, waving good-bye next to Benjamin and Bugsy.

I raised a paw. "Bye, mouselets! I hope to see you soon . . . if we make it back in one piece!"

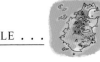

By then, they couldn't see us anymore as we hurtled back in time and space toward **CHARLEMAGNE'S COURT**!

WHAT A RELIEF!

After the usual **shaking**, we saw the usual flash of light. Finally, the Cheese-O-Sphere stopped. The door opened with a *HISS*. Rats, I felt *enormously nauseous* all over again! My fur was a nice green color, like moldy mascarpone.

Ughhhh!

Staggering, I approached the door and peeked out.

WHat a ReLief! We had arrived at Charlemagne's court in Aachen!

Outside, everything seemed peaceful.

Maybe for once we hadn't landed with our tails right smack in the middle of danger! I was overjoyed.

Maybe for once we would get through this time period without the usual complications and the usual trouble!

Thea interrupted my thoughts, showing me her **medieval** costume. "What do you think, Brother? Do I look mousetastic?"

That's when I noticed that we were all wearing outfits from **CHARLEMAGNE'S** time!

Looking at our clothes, I noticed that even Charlemagne's clothes were very simple. His tunic was identical to ours!

FASHION IN CHARLEMAGNE'S TIME

Clothes from the MIDDLE AGES served three main functions: to cover the whole body (no part of the body was to be shown in public!), to protect from the cold, and to decorate the body.

Because of this, most everyone wore cloaks and tunics with big, wide sleeves. WOMEN wore dresses down to their feet with a sash around their waist, and often had a wrap draped over their head or shoulders.

Thea's tunic is quite elegant. It has long, flared sleeves that almost cover her paws.

Geronimo's cloak is ample, refined — and green, of course. It closes on the shoulder with a clip.

Columbus's boots are practical and comfortable, and made of thick leather. They tie with laces at the ankle.

MEN wore two main articles of clothing on their torsos: a tunic with snug sleeves and one with larger sleeves that could be swapped out for a cloak. They wore thin, short pants or trousers that went down to their ankles. The richer men wore shoes and a cloak, too.

Girls, like the daughter of King Charlemagne, often wore their hair in long, gorgeous braids!

Charlemagne always wore a sword with a golden handle full of precious stones. His most famous sword was named Joyeuse.

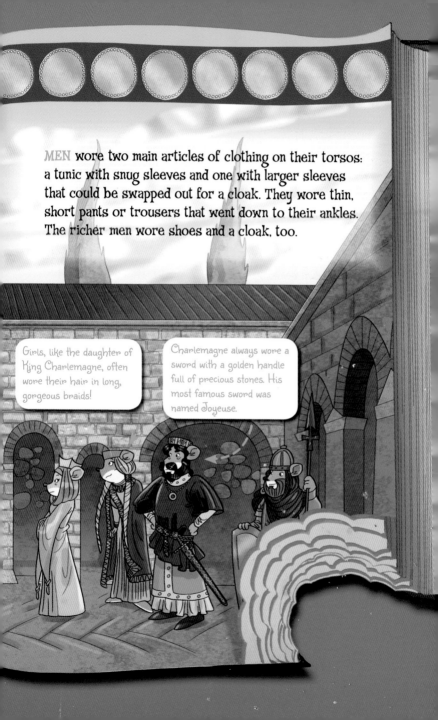

Trap looked at him, confused. "Hey, Charley, where did you put your scepter?"

Charlemagne adjusted his tunic on his shoulders and huffed, "Clothes aren't important! A real king must be comfortable so that he can move quickly and ride on horseback. He must not distinguish himself for the richness of his clothes, but for his valor! I only wear a crown, jewels, and silk clothing during official **occasions**: ceremonies, ambassador visits,

Where did you put your scepter?

Other things are much more important!

and the like. **What a nuisance!**"

Trap shrugged. "Well, if you don't like jewels, fancy clothes, and golden scepters, give them to me. I'll take them off your paws!"

I bowed before Charlemagne and muttered, "Your Majesty, excuse my cousin."

CHARLEMAGNE said good-bye to us with one paw over his heart. "Thank you, friends. I will never forget what you've done for me! If you ever want to come and visit, here is a safe-conduct.* With this, you will be led to me safely!"

I offered him the MEMORY-ERASING ESSENCE so that he would forget his adventure through time.

Charlemagne climbed off the Cheese-O-Sphere and waved good-bye. I closed the door and sat back at the control block. It was time to leave!

"Now we just need to take Christopher

---

* A safe-conduct was a permission form, written and signed by a king or authority, that allowed protection during entrance, exit, and passage through a forbidden territory.

Columbus back!" I squeaked. "Then we can go home, too!"

Thea and Trap cheered, "HOORAY!"

But then the Cheese-O-Sphere began to vibrate.

FRRRRRRRRRRRR!

The walls began to smoke!

Pffffffffffft!

We heard a really loud whistle, like a teakettle boiling.

Tweeeeeeeeeee!

And the Cheese-O-Sphere DISINTEGRATED!

All of a sudden, we were standing in front of Charlemagne's palace at Aachen, covered in cheese fondue from ears to tails!

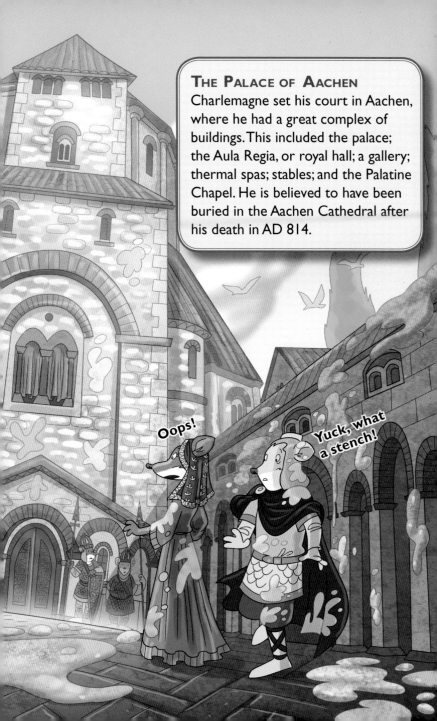

THE PALACE OF AACHEN
Charlemagne set his court in Aachen, where he had a great complex of buildings. This included the palace; the Aula Regia, or royal hall; a gallery; thermal spas; stables; and the Palatine Chapel. He is believed to have been buried in the Aachen Cathedral after his death in AD 814.

CHEESE FONDUE!

"Oh noooo!" I yelled, wiping my snout, which was dripping with cheese.

"Now how will we get home?" Thea cried.

"Yum, cheese fondue!" Trap squeaked, filling his mouth with pawfuls of melted cheese.

Oh, for the love of cheese, my cousin was eating the time machine!

Before I could stop him, we were surrounded by Charlemagne's knights. They pointed lances at us, thundering, "WHO ARE YOU?"

"What are you doing?"

"Where did you come from?"

"What do you want?"

Covering their noses with their paws and poking us with their lances, they forced us to follow them. Right then, I noticed a globe-like mass, almost like a brain made of cheese. It was the quantico-cheeso brain of the Cheese-O-Sphere!

I barely had time to grab it and stick it in the brain carrier, which had miraculously survived! I quickly hid them in a corner.

As I did, a soldier yelled, "Move it, cheesebrain!"

Thea elbowed me and whispered, "Pssst!

Who are you?

What are you doing?

Ack!

You all stink!

Geronimo, pull out the ꕷꕷⴼⴼꕉꕉ-ꕞⴼⴼⴼⴼⴼ!"

I pawed myself in the forehead. "Holey cheese, Thea, why didn't I think of that earlier?"

Rat-munching rattlesnakes, where had I put it? Frantically, I began to search. Finally, I found a piece of scroll at the bottom of my bag. It was all covered in cheese!

I grabbed it with my paw. "Hey, you!" I called to the guards. "That's enough poking at our tails!

Charlemagne,
Emperor of the Holy Roman Empire,
orders that these rodents be allowed
to travel freely throughout the entire
Roman Empire. Whoever stops their
mission will be severely punished!
Signed:
Charlemagne

We have a royal safe-conduct!"

The guards looked at me, confused. "A royal safe-conduct? Give it here, rat!"

Plugging his nose because of the stinky cheese, a guard examined the scroll. Beneath a layer of melted cheese he spotted the royal seal. "Hmmm . . . it really does look like the *royal seal*. Come, **CHARLEMAGNE** will decide what we should do with you rodents!"

Still poking at our tails, the guards LED us to the throne room. There, on a marble throne, Charlemagne sat next to his wife, surrounded by his children and his court.

I was trembling to the very ends of my whiskers.

Would he recognize us or order us to be skewered like cheese-flavored mouse kebabs?

Can I Skewer Them?

Charlemagne stared at us . . . and stared at us . . . and stared at us.

"I think I've seen you all somewhere," he said slowly. "But where? I don't remember having given you a **safe-conduct**! Who are you?"

A knight squeaked up. "My king, can I skewer them? They seem like spies to me. Plus, they **smell** like rotten cheese!"

I **bowed** respectfully. "Your Majesty, we have already met in a place and time very far from here. My name is Geronimardo of Mousetonia, and this is my sister, Theana, and my cousin Trappulot. And this here is the famouse Christopher Columbus, an explorer and navigator."

A buzz went around the room. "Christopher Columbus? He's famouse? I've never heard of him!"

Columbus was clearly very offended, so he said something that could have changed the course of history forever.

"I am VERY famouse! And I will be even more famouse when I discover the new world!"

Everyone burst out **laughing**.

"New world? Forget about it!"

"Ha, ha, ha! Sounds like a delusional cheesebrain to me!"

No one believed him!

Charlemagne lifted his paw. "**Enough!** These rodents are my guests, even if they smell of smoked cheese!"

Then he turned to us. "Mice, you are welcome! My home is your home!"

I **bowed** until my whiskers grazed the ground. "Thank you, Your Majesty! How can we repay your hospitality?"

He scratched his snout THOUGHTFULLY.

"Well, for starters, bathe! No offense, but you smell like rotten cheese! Then you, Geronimardo, you seem intellectual. You will write my biography, along with my trusted Einhard*! You, Theana, will become the tutor** for my mouselets. You seem very wise, and they have a lot to learn. You, Columbus, can be my geographer. I need new **maps** of my kingdom!"

---

* Einhard was a Frankish historian who worked for Charlemagne. He was his official biographer.
** A tutor was the teacher and educator of the young in noble families.

Then he turned to Trap. "And what can you do?"

Trap began to brag. "Modestly speaking, I am a *genius*! I am a food expert, with the record for 'fastest nibbler.' I specialize in jokes, tricks, and pranks of all kinds — especially pranks on my foolish cousin here! And I am also an **INVENTOR**. Do you need fur lotion? A cream to fight calluses? Something to

You're funny, mouse!

Humph!

Huff!

Hee, hee!

Oops!

Hmmm . . .

make your sword **shine**? I, Trappulot of Stiltonia, can handle it!"

Charlemagne burst out laughing. "You're funny, mouse! You will be the **court jester**!"

Charlemagne clapped his paws, satisfied. "Good, good, good! Now each of you get to work, because the early mouse gets the **cheese**! Right, Mother?"

Next to him was an elderly rodent with an energetic smile. "Absolutely, **get to work**! There's a kingdom to govern, conspiracies to stop, and an empire to control!"

To work! Now!

Come on, let's go!

Everyone — courtesans, counts, marquis, stable hands, valets, dames and damsels, servants, countesses, and knights — darted out to put their paws to work!

I couldn't help giggling. The queen mother reminded me of Grandfather William, always shouting out orders!

I suddenly felt NOSTALGIC for home. Would we ever get back to New Mouse City now that the Cheese-O-Sphere had exploded? I had managed to save the quantico-cheeso brain, so maybe all was not lost?

Run!

To work!

Quick

At once!

EVERYONE TO THE HOT SPRINGS

My friends and I were about to leave the room when Charlemagne **thundered**, "You all come with me. We're going to the hot springs! You can bathe there!"

I turned **red** with embarrassment, but Trap sang softly, "We smell of cheese, me and my throng, but actually we are quite strong! The strongest one is me! Trappulot deedle dee!"

Deedle dee!

A perfect jester!

Before I could shake a whisker, Trap began to walk on his hands! He really was a marvemouse **court jester**!

As we headed to the springs, King Charlemagne said, "There's nothing better than a nice **BATH** in the springs, believe me! It can give you ideas, relax you, and most importantly . . . get rid of that rotten **cheese smell**!"

And that's how Charlemagne subjected us to a crazy treatment of:

1) a bath in hot **sulfur** water (*which stunk of rotten eggs!*)

2) purifying **mud** compresses (*which stunk of swamp sludge!*)

3) a massage with fresh **hay** (*which had nettles in it!*)

4) and, finally, a (*too*) vigorous massage with scented oils to get rid of the **cheese smell**!

The **worst** part was that Charlemagne told

me stories about his life the whole time. I even had to take notes!

Charlemagne kept asking, "So, did you write it down, mouse? Are you sure you know how to *write*? You're an intellectual mouse, right?"

To be honest, I was not such an expert at writing with a feather pen on a scroll. Plus, my paws were soapy! The pen kept slipping and leaving terrible **ink stains**.

When I passed my NOTES to Einhard, Charlemagne's official biographer, he shook his snout. "You really write terribly! This looks like chicken scratch."

Cock-a-doodle doo!

CHARLEMAGNE

CHARLES I (AD 742–814) was called Charlemagne. He was the son of Pepin the Short, king of the Franks, and conquered the Pannonian Avars, the Danes, the Slavs, the Saxons, and the Bavarians.

After rejecting DESIDERATA (daughter of Desiderius, King of the Lombards), he had to fight Desiderius. He defeated him and took control of the Lombard territory in Italy.

On Christmas night in the year AD 800, CHARLEMAGNE WAS CROWNED emperor of the Holy Roman Empire by Pope Leo III. That is how he rebuilt the political unity of the west.

THE CORONATION

THE PALATINE SCHOOL

CHARLEMAGNE was not well educated, but he did know the importance of culture. He recruited the best intellectuals of the time (Einhard, Alcuin of York, Paul the Deacon) to surround him. He also founded various SCHOOLS to educate the young, including the Palatine School, located in the Aachen court.

In these new cultural centers, ancient manuscripts were copied and then entrusted to the monks.

In honor of Charlemagne, this new type of writing became known as CAROLINGIAN MINUSCULE. It was simpler, and made copying classic texts easier.

Charlemagne also introduced FEUDALISM, a system for managing and controlling the empire. Under feudalism, the sovereign gave his subjects fiefdoms (land) to govern, in exchange for loyalty and military protection. Whoever gained a fiefdom became a VASSAL and had other subjects beneath him, VAVASORS.

Squeak, I looked like such a cheesebrain!

Einhard forced me to recopy the same page a thousand times until it was **perfect**.

I thought my paw was going to fall off!

In the end, my writing really looked like a *calligraphy* masterpiece in pure Carolingian minuscule.

But I had writer's cramp, blisters, FLAMING PAWS, and bloodshot eyes!

Ow, my paws are on fire!

Cheesy cream puffs, the life of an intellectual during **CHARLEMAGNE'S** time was harder than a hunk of Parmesan!

When I was reunited with my friends, I was a mousely **MESS**.

In Charlemagne's time, every BOOK required a great deal of work. Someone had to prepare each scroll, copy the text by hand, decorate it, and bind the pages. Producing books was very costly! Only the nobles could afford private libraries.

Charlemagne encouraged education and the production of more books, and supported the use of CAROLINGIAN MINUSCULE, which was more legible and easier to read.

THE NEW CHEESE-O-SPHERE!

When we returned to the palace, Thea asked, "Now how will we get home?"

"Stay calm," I said. "I have the **quantico-cheeso brain**!"

"Maybe we have a chance of getting out of here after all," Thea said. "Professor von Volt connected us directly to the brain, remember?"

I'll handle it!

Heeeelp!

WE WERE RETURNING TO THE PALACE WHEN

...I ACCIDENTALLY STEPPED IN HORSE MANURE AND FLEW THROUGH THE AIR

Trap groaned. "Ugh, we still have to build a new **time machine**. We need something that will protect us during our journey through time!"

"You're right, Trap," I said. "We need to use something big, solid, and easy to transport."

Right then, I **stepped** in some horse manure, did a spectacular flip in the air, and landed snoutfirst in a barrel full of **dirty** water! Rats!

Splash!

I found it!

I ENDED UP SNOUTFIRST   AND HAD A MOUSETASTIC IDEA!

As soon as I popped up, I cried, "I found it!"

Then I lowered my voice, so no one could hear me. "Psssst . . . Pssst . . . psssst . . . psst! Psst pssst . . . pssst . . . barrel . . . psst pssst . . . pssst . . . pssst . . . psst pssst . . . pssst . . . silence . . . psst pssst . . . pssst . . . tonight . . . pssst . . . at midnight . . . pssst . . . pssst . . . pssst . . . psst! Understand?"

Then we split up. Each of us returned to our jobs for the rest of the day so no one would suspect that anything unusual was happening.

I was a little sad to leave Charlemagne's time, but we needed to complete our mission! So that night, at the stroke of midnight, we all gathered in the court of the Aachen palace in secret.

The barrel of dirty water was still there. Together, we pushed it over and emptied it out. Then we tried to be quiet as we rolled it outside the palace!

We recovered the quantico-cheeso brain, and when we were sure that no one could hear, all four of us **climbed** into the barrel!

Trap convinced me to get in first, so I ended up with Thea's paw on my tail! Columbus stuck a paw in my eye, and Trap elbowed me in the ear! **Squeeak, we were squished like sardines!**

"Argh, you're crushing me!" I hissed. "Say the destination, quick!"

Thea announced, "Destination: Columbus's flagship vessel!"

Will we make it?

Fingers crossed!

Who knows?

Beats me!

DESTINATION:

COLUMBUS'S VOYAGE TO AMERICA

RATS TRAVELING ON SOMEONE ELSE'S DIME!

For a moment, nothing happened. We all held our **BREATH**. Would the quantico-cheeso brain bring us to Christopher Columbus's time even without the **Cheese-O-Sphere**? Would our makeshift time machine work . . . or not?

There was only one way to find out. We had to wait and see!

Squeak, my whiskers were wobbling from the stress!

What a feline fright!

Finally, after what felt like forever, there was a FLASH of light (that was smaller than usual), a BANG (that was a lot less powerful than usual), and we began to spin and spin and spin. But this time, on top of all the spinning, our time machine began to bang us all over the place! UP AND DOWN! FORWARD AND BACKWARD!

We were banged, rattled, and completely dazed!

THEN OUR TIME MACHINE LANDED.

Unfortunately, it wasn't a soft landing. We definitely bruised our tails! YOUCH!

Finally, there was a hiss, and we were surrounded by a light fog. I lifted the cover of the BARREL and stuck out my snout. We were in the cargo hold of an ancient ship that swayeD back anD forth.

I jumped out of the barrel and squeaked with joy. "Holey cheese, we did it!"

Just then, I heard voices coming from the bottom of the ship's cargo hold. "**ADMIRAL**, is that you? Where are you? We've been looking for you for hours!"

I quickly hid behind the barrel alongside Thea, Trap, and Columbus. Then I gave Columbus a spoonful of the **MEMORY-ERASING ESSENCE**. "Quick, Columbus, sir — drink this!"

Hooray!

He whispered, "Friends, I know that in a moment I will no longer remember you, or this fantastic and bizarre adventure! Before I drink this horribly stinky potion, I want to say thank you for all you've done for me!"

Columbus plugged his

nose and barely had enough time to swallow the **MEMORY-ERASING ESSENCE** before two sailors as big as barrels approached, shining their lanterns on us and thundering, "What do I see here? Three rats traveling on someone else's dime? You can't do that!"

One of them rubbed his paws together.

"Compliments, **Admiral Columbus**! You dug up three freeloaders! Can we throw them in the sea? Or abandon them on a **deserted** island? Leave them to us — we'll take care of them!"

Columbus **stared and stared and stared** at

What have we here!

Three rats traveling on someone else's dime!

us, but he couldn't quite put his paw on who we were. The memory-erasing essence had already taken effect!

Trap, Thea, and I all looked at one another, **WORRIED**. What would Columbus say? Our fates were in his paws!

ALL ABOARD THE SANTA MARÍA!

The sailors **GRABBED** us by the tails and dragged us to the deck.

We were aboard the Santa María, the flagship vessel of Columbus's fleet! Our mission was almost over. We just had to find the right time to return to our makeshift **time machine** and get back to New Mouse City. We were so close!

I tried to remember what I had learned about Columbus landing in America so I could predict the right moment for us to get our **tails in gear**. If only I had the Super Manual with me, or at least Bugsy and Benjamin — they were studying this

CHRISTOPHER COLUMBUS

CHRISTOPHER COLUMBUS

was born in Genoa, Italy, in AD 1451.
He was the son of a Genovese textile
worker. From the time he was young,
he proved himself to be a skilled
navigator. Columbus was passionate
about geography and dedicated himself
to commercial sea travel. In 1476, he
moved to PORTUGAL, where he married Filipa Moniz.

In the fifteenth century, the only other lands known to
Europeans included part of Asia and NORTHERN AFRICA.
Columbus was determined to reach the Indies by traveling
westward, instead of taking the regular eastward route.

After King John II of Portugal refused to fund his project,
Columbus moved to Spain, where he received support from
FERDINAND AND ISABELLA of Castile.

With three ships (THE NIÑA, THE PINTA, AND THE SANTA
MARÍA), Columbus and his crew set sail from Palos on
August 3, 1492, en route to the Indies on an uncharted course.
On October 12, it is believed that they landed on the Island of
Guanahani in the Bahamas, which Columbus called San Salvador.

Other trips followed, in which Columbus touched on many of
the Caribbean islands. Columbus died in 1506, never realizing
that he had landed on America.

subject in school! I thought hard about the last time I had helped Benjamin with his homework . . .

We were somewhere in the middle of the **ocean**, but I didn't have a clue how much longer the journey would be!

I politely asked, "Excuse me, what day is today?"

The **BIGGER** of the two sailors hissed in my ear. "Today is October eleventh, rat! But for you, it's the day you get eaten by sharks, *hee, hee*!"

Admiral Columbus kept staring at us, muttering, "**Hmmm!** What am I going to do with you?"

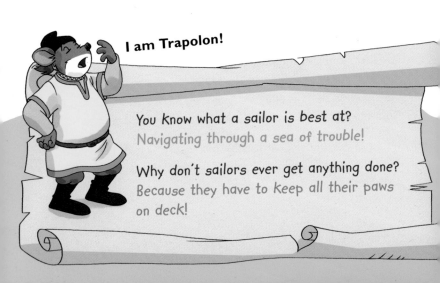

I am Trapolon!

You know what a sailor is best at?
Navigating through a sea of trouble!

Why don't sailors ever get anything done?
Because they have to keep all their paws on deck!

Trap interrupted him. "My name is Trapolon de Stilton Cheesyon. If you would consider it, I could be your personal chef, or perhaps lift your SPIRITS with some jokes."

One of the sailors put up a paw for silence. "Enough squeaking, you FREELOADING rat! I'll throw you overboard!"

Columbus stopped him. "Don't touch this rat. I need him alive! This trip is long and boring — he will cheer me up with his little stories."

Trap stuck his tongue out at me. "I got hired and you didn't! Na na na-na na!"

The BIGGER sailor grumbled, "Ugh, can we at least throw these other two overboard?"

"Are you sewer rats or sailors?" Columbus squeaked. "Put them down at once! They will work to pay for their trip!"

Then he turned to Thea and me. "What can you two do?"

Thea said, "My name is Theabella de Stilton Cheesyon. I will give you a short demonstration of my skills! I need a **VOLUNTEER** . . ."

She looked around, then pointed to the two biggest sailors. "You, come here!"

Before anyone could squeak, she did a skilled karate move. "Haiii-yaaa!"

She hit that **loudmouthed** sailor in his undertail!

THEA CALLED ON SOME VOLUNTEERS SO SHE COULD DEMONSTRATE HER SKILLS . . .

THEN SHE DID A SKILLED KARATE MOVE — AND HIT ONE MOUSE RIGHT IN HIS TAIL!

He went flying upside down into a barrel full of **FISH**.

"Would you like another demonstration, or is that enough?" Thea asked the sailor sweetly. "Do you still want to throw us **overboard**?"

Columbus looked at her with admiration. "Madam, you are hired! **YOU WILL BE MY BODYGUARD!**"

Finally, Columbus turned to me. "You, what

Splash!

THE SAILOR FLEW UPSIDE DOWN INTO A BARREL FULL OF FISH!

can you do? I don't really see you as a **BODYGUARD**. You don't look like much of a musclemouse."

I wasn't sure what to say. Rats! "Well . . . I am Geronimon de Stilton and all the other things they said. And, let's see. What can I do? I don't know much about ships, but I know how to do a lot of other things . . . a little of this, and a little of that . . . and I know a bit about books . . ."

Columbus put up a paw. "I will make you a do-it-all shipmouse! To begin, you will give the deck a nice scrubbing, then you will do the laundry,

Umm, I . . .

What can you do?

mend my clothing, and lend a paw in the kitchen. And since you know a thing or two about *books*, you will dust the library, too. But first, you need to change. You're wearing **ridiculous** clothes! Did you come from a costume party?"

The sailor looked Columbus up and down. "Admiral, were you at that costume **party** as well?"

That's when Columbus decided to loan us some **clothes** from his wardrobe. We were finally dressed in the Spanish fashions of the time.

FASHION IN COLUMBUS'S TIME

From the 1400s to the middle of the 1500s, wealthy European WOMEN wore dresses made of fine and heavy fabrics, like damask, brocade, and silk velvet, with flower patterns and threads of gold and silver, embroidered with pearls or PRECIOUS STONES. The dresses had deep necklines. The waist was narrowed by a CORSET, and the skirt was large and voluminous.

A pink silk velvet dress with a low-necked corset. The big, regal cloak is decorated with fur.

Your Majesty . . .

This coat has thick fur trim that is naturally dyed. It is worn with fitted leggings.

The MEN wore elegant coats with lined, fitted sleeves. These coats covered the torso and reached halfway down the thigh.

Underneath, men wore a short TUNIC buttoned in the front with fitted pants or colored stockings.

Thea is wearing a damask dress with large sleeves. Her light-colored shirt shows through the long slits.

Queen Isabella of Castile!

What charm!

Geronimo's hat is very refined! It is made of velvet and has a lined brim.

GERONIMON HERE, GERONIMON THERE!

I soon discovered that the life of a do-it-all was ROUGH! First, I began to **scrub** the deck with soapy water. Trap walked by with Columbus, *yelling* out jokes. Then he "slipped" and kicked me in the **TAIL**! I ended up with my snout in the bucket! Squeak!

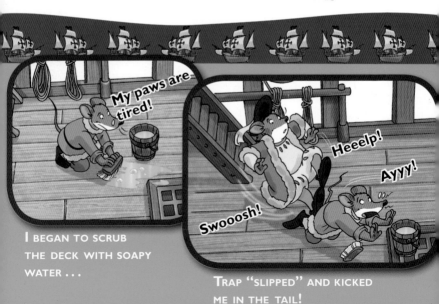

My paws are tired!

Heeelp!

Ayyy!

Swoooosh!

I BEGAN TO SCRUB THE DECK WITH SOAPY WATER . . .

TRAP "SLIPPED" AND KICKED ME IN THE TAIL!

I struggled to my paws. I tried to pull off the bucket that had gotten stuck on my snout, but I set a **PAW** on the soapy broom and ended up hitting my head on the mast. Squeak, what a blow!

Holey cheese, the life of a do-it-all was ROUGH!

Everyone was squeaking at me. "Geronimon, clean **here**! Geronimon, slide over **there**! Geronimon, go up! Geronimon, come down!"

I was about to yank out my whiskers!

Plop!

Argh!

...BUT I SLIPPED AND HIT MY HEAD ON THE MAST!

I TRIED TO PULL OFF THE BUCKET ...

Bang!

I ENDED UP WITH MY SNOUT IN THE BUCKET!

I washed the entire crew's dirty socks (*which were super-stinky, like rotten cheese rinds!*).

I **REORGANIZED** the bunks (*which were so dirty that all kinds of fleas, bedbugs, and lice lived there!*).

FAMILY OF FLEAS

I **polished** the 987 rings on the anchor's chain (*which were encrusted with algae and mussels that smelled like rotten fish!*).

I **HELPED** the cook prepare slop for the whole crew (*which reeked like rotten cabbage!*).

ROTTEN CABBAGE SLOP

Oh yes, the life of a do-it-all was ROUGH!

I did find a **blossoming** twig caught on the anchor chain, which meant that land was close! I tucked it into my pocket to show Columbus later.

As I was working, **NO ONE** paid me any attention, so I could hear the crew chattering.

On the deck, I heard two sailors mutter, "Ugh, I can't take sailing anymore. I think the admiral is telling us **tales**!"

In the dormitory, two cabin mice were complaining. "Will we ever get there? I think we're lost!"

In the kitchen, the cook was **WHINING** to the helper. "For the love of cheese, there's no more food. I think the crew is going to rebel!"

Cheese and crackers, this was a **SUPER-SERIOUS** situation!

I promised myself I would talk to Admiral Columbus as soon as possible.

NIGHT had fallen by the time I knocked on the door of Admiral Columbus's quarters. A voice answered me between sobs. "**SIGH! SOB!** Come in . . ."

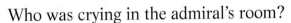

Who was crying in the admiral's room?

I pushed the door open — and saw that the rodent crying was Christopher Columbus himself!

Thea was standing next to him. "You try, Geronimon! I can't seem to console him!"

Trap was there, too. "It's serious!" he squeaked. "My jokes aren't even making him **LAUGH**!"

Tears poured down Columbus's snout. "I can't do it! I've failed — we'll never make it to the Indies!"

"Admiral, don't worry! I promise that tomorrow, you will land in Amer — I mean — umm . . . in the Indies!" I said.

Columbus's **EYES** widened. "How do you know? Are you some sort of seer?"

Swiss cheese on rye, I had slipped up! What could I say so Columbus wouldn't realize that I was from the **FUTURE**?

LAND! LAND! LAAAAND!

I smiled. "I am a do-it-all, and one of the things I can do is really important: **read**! I've read a lot of books, and I discovered that if you see **FLOWERY** twigs floating in the sea, it means that you are near land. And I have one here! I found it this morning as I was **polishing** the anchor's chain!"

When he saw the twig, Columbus stopped crying. "Thank you, Geronimon! Now I know we will reach **LAND** soon!"

I patted him on the shoulder. "Quick, Admiral, gather the **CREW** and announce that we are about to arrive in Amer — I mean — in the Indies!"

Then I **LOWERED** my voice. "I must

warn you: The sailors are fed up. They're about to rebel!"

In a flash, Columbus was on deck, gathering the crew.

"Sailors, friends!" he called. "Don't get your tails in a twist — tomorrow morning at dawn, we will reach land!"

Tomorrow, we will reach land!

The sailors threw up their paws. "Admiral, you've been telling us the same story every day for a month: 'We'll arrive tomorrow! Land is near!'"

The crew all started squeaking at once.

"Enough! We're fed up!"

"We want to go home!"

"We can't take the sea anymore!"

"We can't take the waves anymore!"

"We can't take the cabbage soup anymore!"

Columbus lifted his paw and thundered, "Silence! This time it's different! I have

We're fed up! Fed up, fed up! The most fed up! So enormously fed up!

proof — look, a blossoming twig. Geronimon found it **tangled** in the anchor! This means land is near. Now, everyone, off to sleep! If we don't reach land tomorrow, I give you my rodent's word of honor that I will take you back **HOME** at once!"

Angry squeaks turned to cheers. "Hooray, Christopher Columbus! Hooray, Geronimon!"

The ship was **silent** as everyone scampered off to try and sleep. But not a single rodent closed an eye that **NIGHT**. We were all too excited!

Before dawn, there was an echo throughout the ship: **"LAND! LAND! LAAAAND!"**

Just a few hours later, our paws touched land*!

It was dawn on October 12, 1492!

Thundering cattails, I was thrilled. This was a famousely important *moment* — it would change history forever!

Thea prodded me. "Geronimo, no one is paying

---

* Christopher Columbus landed on an island in the Bahamas on October 12, 1492. He called it San Salvador.

any attention to us! Quick, let's scamper down to the cargo hold. It's time to go home!"

In a flash, we ran off to our "time machine."

Unfortunately, someone had filled the barrel with rotten cabbage cores! What a stench! Yuck! We plugged our noses and yelled out our last destination: "To New Mouse City: Professor von Volt's laboratory!"

RETURN TO
NEW MOUSE CITY!

FINALLY HOME!
OR MAYBE NOT?

As soon as we uttered our destination, there was the usual *FLASH OF LIGHT* and the usual **BANG**. Then the "time machine" took off. As usual, we began to shake like cheese smoothies and my face instantly turned **GREEN**! Moldy mozzarella, my poor stomach!

I consoled myself by thinking that this was the last time I'd have to go through this. Our mission was **complete**. Soon, we would be back in New Mouse City, in Professor von Volt's **LABORATORY**!

Just then, there was another bang, even louder than the first!

BANG!

Our "time machine" disintegrated around us!

Squeeeak, what a feline fright!

At that moment, I saw the **quantico-cheeso** brain next to me.

Holey cheese, that's all that was left of the **Cheese-O-Sphere**!

I grabbed it with one paw and clung to it desperately. "**Heeeelp!**"

Thea looked over at me. "Hang on — we'll try to reach you!"

"Cousin, don't let go," Trap hollered, "or we'll keep faaaalling!"

Trap and Thea grabbed on to my paws, and I held on to the quantico-cheeso brain as tight as I could!

We were like three shipwrecked mice clinging to wreckage, lost in the ocean of time and space! HOW scary! HOW frightful! HOW Mousetastically terrifying!

Would we survive, or be demousified? Would we arrive home, or would we be lost forever?

After what seemed like forever, there was a FLASH OF LIGHT.

I thought we would disintegrate . . . but then I landed on my tail on the floor of Professor von Volt's laboratory!

I barely had enough time to squeak, "W-we're s-saved!"

THEN everything went black, and I fainted.

When I finally came to, I found myself in the relaxation zone of the INCREDIBLE AIRSHIP, which was equipped with everything a mouse could want. I was lying down on a super-squishy bed, covered by a comforter as SOFT as a cloud. There was some sweet, relaxing music in the background, with sounds of water flowing and birds chirping . . .

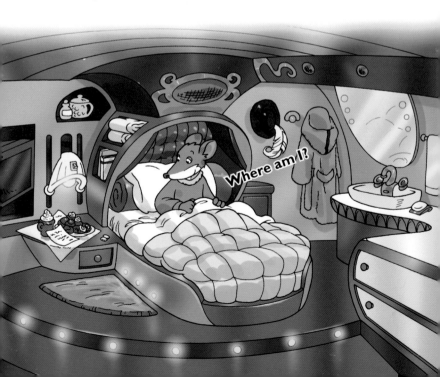

On the nightstand next to me was a bowl of Cheesy Chews and a cup filled with Gorgonzola hot **chocolate**, with a tuft of whipped cream and white chocolate grated on top. There were pastries with cheese and nuts, cheese-stuffed cookies, even a slice of cheesecake. Yum!

Next to the food, there was a note:

WELCOME BACK, GERONIMO!
WHEN YOU WAKE UP, MEET US
IN THE MEETING ROOM.
SIGNED, YOUR FRIEND,
PROFESSOR VON VOLT

SLURP!

I gobbled up all the delicious things the professor had left for me. Yum!

Cheese niblets, I immediately felt better!

Then I took a nice hot bath in the Jacuzzi with Parmesan salts. Finally, I put on the **CLOTHES** that Professor von Volt had left out for me — a **comfortable** sweat suit in my favorite color, dark green!

How delicious!

I TASTED A FEW TREATS . . .

I peeked in the mirror. I looked good, refreshed, and rested, like a mouse on vacation! I looked at myself again. Hey, not bad! *I was in shape!* I could even see a few little muscles. Traveling through time, despite all the scares, had done me some good. Now I was ready to meet the others.

I **headed** to the meeting room, **LOOKING** for Professor von Volt, Thea, and Trap.

When he **SAW** me coming, the professor ran to meet me. "Geronimo, MY FRIEND, how are you feeling?"

Thea hugged me tight. "Thanks, Brother — you saved our fur!"

For once, Trap didn't even **flick** my ear. He didn't make fun of me, or

THEN I TOOK A HOT BATH . . .

How relaxing!

Stylish!

FINALLY, I PUT ON THE COMFORTABLE SWEAT SUIT.

pull any pranks. He just said one word: "Thanks!"

I shrugged. "I didn't do anything special. I just stayed **STUCK** to the quantico-cheeso brain like glue! You all would have done the same for me, right?"

Trap **FLiCKeD** my ear. Rats! "Of course, of course! But enough with all this **SWEETNESS**, it's making my teeth hurt. Now for more serious things — when do we eat?

Thanks!

Thanks, Brother!

I'm so hungry, it feels like I haven't eaten since Columbus landed on **AMERICA**!"

I burst out laughing. Trap was back to normal. I love my cousin just the way he is . . . even if he's always playing annoying pranks on me!

At that point, I turned to the professor and muttered, embarrassed, "Umm, Professor? The Cheese-O-Sphere . . . there was an **incident**. I'm sorry! It did some fabumouse work for us, but . . . unfortunately . . . regrettably . . . as you may have guessed . . . it's destroyed! Disintegrated!

Enough sweetness!

Flick!

Argh!

There's nothing left, just cheese fondue!"

The professor interrupted me. "Oh, Geronimo! I'm the one who should apologize to you! Unfortunately, the Cheese-O-Sphere couldn't stand up to the SPATIO-TEMPORAL friction. The pure Gorgonzolion molecules could not handle the gravitational impact of the electro-decheesifying charge! Can you forgive me? You were about to lose your fur! I never should have sent you on a mission before I finished testing the Cheese-O-Sphere."

I sighed. "It's a shame that there's nothing left of the Cheese-O-Sphere."

The professor looked at Thea and Trap like he had a secret. "Something is left, Geronimo!"

Just then, I felt something sniffing my outfit . . .

I spun on my paws and saw something that looked like a strange, cheese-shaped animal!

Professor von Volt explained, "The Cheese-O-Sphere's quantico-cheeso brain survived, and during the **EXPLOSION**, something mousetastic happened — it connected with its brain, and now it has real emotions!"

"Huh? What?" I couldn't wrap my mind around what the professor was squeaking!

What is it?

That strange cheese kept jumping around me, **wagging its tail**, and slurping.

"Slurp! Slurp!"

Fabumouse!

The quantico-cheeso brain had come to life — it had become a cheese **CUB**!

Thea laughed. "You know, Geronimo, he seems to like you. He's been at the foot of your bed the whole time. We named him CHeezum! Isn't he cute?"

Sniff, sniff!

Cheezum jumped up into my arms, slurping my snout with melted cheese licks.

SLURP, SLURP, SLURP!

"Hey, hold on, you're wetting my whiskers!" I grumbled. But I really didn't mind. I knew I had made a new friend!

Slow down, you're wetting my whiskers!

Slurp, slurp!

A New Agenda!

A few days later, we headed home. Everything was back to normal — mousehole, work, newsroom, writing . . .

Finally, Saturday afternoon rolled around again. I was ready to start up my **A.A.A.A.** (Amazing Agenda for an **AWESOME AFTERNOON**!) exactly where I had been interrupted the week before, when I left for my journey through time. I was going to

Finally!

Geronimo's **A.A.A.A.**

1. Laaaze aaaaround until laaaate!
2. Have an aaaafternoon snaaaack of aaaaged Aaaasiago!
3. Relaaaax in my paaaawchair (in front of my faaaavorite TV show)!
4. Get some aaaair in the paaaark!

start with **#3:** Relax in my pawchair, in front of my favorite TV show!

I was already *lounging* in the pawchair with the remote in my paw when the doorbell rang. It was Benjamin and Bugsy!

"Uncle G!" Bugsy yelled, making my ears **ring**.

"We missed you, Uncle Geronimo!" Benjamin exclaimed, jumping into my arms.

"I missed you, too, mouselets!" I squeaked.

Uncle Geronimo!

"How are you?"

"We're fabumouse, thanks! All thanks to Aunt Sweetfur, who got us back on our paws with a super-concentrated cure of cuddles and treats."

"Oh, good!" I said with a relieved sigh. "I'm so glad. What can I do for you? Do you want a snack? I have some Gorgonzola-and-cream cake in the fridge . . ."

Benjamin and Bugsy looked at each other, grinning.

"We don't have time for a snack now," Benjamin said. "Come with us — we have a surprise for you!"

"Hurry, Uncle G!" Bugsy added, pulling on my paw.

I didn't want to **disappoint** them, so I put my A.A.A.A. on hold.

Family always comes first!

(Plus, I could pick up with my **A.A.A.A.**

later on.)

I turned off the TV, took off my slippers, and got ready to leave.

As soon as we got outside, Benjamin and Bugsy **BLINDFOLDED** me, grabbed my paws, and dragged me all over the city. "We can't wait to show you the surprise, Uncle G! It's going to be **MOUSERIFIC**!"

wondering, *Where they are bringing me? What kind of surprise is this?*

Still blindfolded, I entered a room full of rodents. I could tell, because the room was filled with squeaks and giggles.

"Psst . . . pssst! There he is! Quiet! Pssst . . . surprise . . . ha, ha, ha! Keep it down . . . hee, hee, hee!"

When I opened my eyes, I found myself in a movie theater. I was in the front row, and all

my friends, relatives, and coworkers from The Rodent's Gazette were there. Even Professor von Volt and his family!

Then Benjamin said, "Are you ready, Uncle Geronimo?"

Holey cheese!

I was certainly surprised . . .

I was so surprised that I almost fainted!

Do you want to know why?

How strong!

Wow!

Look, that's Geronimo!

What a feline fright!

the adventures of my last journey through time! I saw the T. rex chase from the **Cretaceous period**, the furious Trojan warriors who wanted to skewer me like mouse kebabs, and the troop of **Huns** with their menacing arrows.

It felt like I was really there! Squeak, what a feline fright!

There were snacks after the movie, but my stomach was still in knots. I was paler than a ball of FRESH MOZZARELLA!

Professor von Volt grinned. "So, Geronimo, did you like the surprise?"

Benjamin and Bugsy squeaked enthusiastically, "Mouserific, right, Uncle G?"

My paws were shaking. "Oh, y-y-yes! It was v-v-very realistic — maybe too realistic!

How did you manage that, Professor? It's impossible to make a movie in just a week!"

Professor von Volt *laughed*. "This isn't a movie, dear Geronimo! These are the images that were recorded by your memory and copied into the **quantico-cheeso** brain when you were sticking to it like glue!"

Cheese and crackers, no wonder it all seemed so **REAL**! That was when the quantico-cheeso brain had **tURneD** into Cheezum.

Just then, Cheezum jumped in my arms and slurped my snout, covering me with melted cheese!

SLURP! SLURP!

Thanks to the quantico-cheeso brain — I mean, **Cheezum** — journey through time had become a mouserific film! Everyone in New Mouse City went to **SEE IT** and relived our exciting adventures through time with us.

It was a **FABUMOUSE** success, and I was so honored to be a part of it, or my name's not Stilton, *Geronimo Stilton*!

Don't miss a single fabumouse adventure!

Up Next: